THE WISH MECHANICS

by Daniel Braum

ISBN: 978-88-99569-52-5

Copyright (Edition) ©2017 Independent Legions Publishing

Copyright (Text) ©Daniel Braum

1° edition paperback July 2017

Editing: Jodi Renée Lester

Cover Art: George C. Cotronis

DEDICATION

For my dad.

SUMMARY

INTRODUCTION 11

HOW TO MAKE LOVE AND NOT TURN TO STONE 16

AN AMERICAN GHOST IN ZURICH 44

THE WATER DRAGON 73

A MAN'S GUIDE TO COSTUMES AND THE MOST COMMON 100
WAYS TO GET ARRESTED (written with Jason Sileo)

RED LIGHTS 125

CANOPY CRAWLERS 134

THE WISH MECHANICS 149

RESOLUTION SEVENTEEN 180

TEA IN THE SAHARA 200

TETSUYA AND THE RANAGAREET 223

THE TRUTH ABOUT PLANET X 255

THIS IS THE SOUND OF YOUR DREAMS DYING 272

ABOUT THE AUTHOR 303
ACKNOWLEDGMENTS 309
FORTHCOMING BOOKS 311
AVAILABLE BOOKS 313

"How to Make Love and Not Turn to Stone" previously published in *The Beauty of Death* (Independent Legions, 2016)

"An American Ghost in Zurich" previously published in *Savage Beasts* (Grey Matter Press, 2015)

"The Water Dragon" previously published in *Yeti. Tiger. Dragon.* (Dim Shores Press, 2016)

"Canopy Crawlers" previously published in *Full Unit Hook Up* #6 (2004)

"The Wish Mechanics" previously published in *Full Unit Hook Up* #9 (2008)

"Tea in the Sahara" previously published in *Kaleidetrope Magazine* (2012)

"Tetsuya and the Ranagareet" previously published in *Strange, Weird and Wonderful Magazine* (2010)

Daniel Braum

The Wish Mechanics

INTRODUCTION

Who, or what, are Wish Mechanics?

Are Wish Mechanics mechanisms by which we collectively, or individually, bring wishes into being?

Is a Wish Mechanic an expert in his or her field? An artisan, of anything, so adept at his or her craft that to the untrained eye his or her ways appear to be magic?

Is a Wish Mechanic one who seeks to bring a vision into being?

Parents. Publishers. Storytellers. Each with their own brand of mad alchemy they transmute experiences from remote corners of the wide world and or just around the corner into tales, stories, spells, hopes, and wishes meant to live again on the page and in the minds and lives of others.

I hope after reading these stories you will answer the question, and tell me.

There are so many labels, categories, and genres and sub-genres for our stories. I've always preferred the term fiction. As a child those were the tales where anything could happen. During most of the fifteen-year period over which most of these stories were written I was either ignorant of or deliberately ignoring genre lines. Muse, imagination, and a desire to share were enough to bring these stories to be.

If you are reading this introduction I figure there is a good chance you might be wondering what to expect from this strange book, of strange tales, from an unknown author, and just what kind of stories you will find here.

I hope you will tell me. It isn't that I don't want to say. It isn't that I don't care, although I do admit my process is not to know or care when I imagine them. What matters most to me is that you enjoy them as much as I do. Learning about the structures and history of the various genres has been an enjoyable new pursuit for me. I've learned enough to know that although there are relations in style, structure, and theme, the stories in this book do not fit neatly into the literary horror or weird fiction label associated with my debut collection *The Night Marchers and Other Strange Tales*. Thus this book operates as both a wonderful pairing and a departure.

Are there science fiction stories here?

Well some of them have rocket ships and things from space and worlds beyond this one.

Are there fantasy stories here?

Well, in some of them there might be dragons of sorts, or people carry swords or go on mad adventures, and there are some very strange trees.

Are there horror stories here?

Well, they are all very dark, they don't always end well, and there are dead people and things that might be ghosts and demons.

You'll find something to enjoy here if you are fond of the *Twilight Zone* and if you delight in things interstitial, tales that defy classification, or stories that mix and operate in between and beyond the boundaries of genre.

The stories original to this collection are "A Man's Guide to Costumes and the Most Common Ways to Get Arrested," "Red Lights," "Resolution Seventeen," "The Truth About Planet X," and "This Is the Sound of Your Dreams Dying.

All of the strange tales in this book are dark and dangerous. They don't necessarily have happy endings. They have a strong sense of setting and place, even if the place is somewhere impossible, far away, or one that exists no longer.

Be ready to move through darkness. There are grand, impersonal, and often uncaring forces at play.

On the journey I hope you will also see the Love. Magic. Mystery. And Wonder that I have seen. And maybe you'll even notice an overlooked wish or two.

Daniel Braum
New York, February 11, 2017

HOW TO MAKE LOVE
AND NOT TURN TO STONE

Michaela sits on the cliff listening to the waves crash on the rocks below, near where the basilisks crawl. The eight-foot reptiles do not like to climb the three-hundred-foot jagged rock wall, although occasionally one does and finds its way into Francois's garden, leaving a trail of tail tracks and petrified deer and squirrels and field mice. Mostly the basilisks like to lounge in the cliffside caves during the heat of day venturing out at night for reasons of their own. Michaela knows the lizards' habits, and immunity to each other's gazes must serve mundane purposes, but she doesn't know what and can't help but assign a mystic significance to their behavior, although she can't put her finger on what that might be either. Francois keeps the stone animals as lawn sculptures, sick fuck that he is, which is part of why she loves him so. She'd very much like to go down to the beach with him and take him in the soft, white sand, basilisks and all, but for now sitting atop the cliff waiting for the bats will do.

"See any yet?" Francois asks.

"No," Michaela says.

Dusk's last light is almost gone and the sky's evening blues are darkening in a way they both find beautiful.

"Maybe they're not hungry," Francois says. "Or they feel the storm coming."

The folding chairs they sit in are close enough that they could touch hands if they wanted to. The sleeves of Michaela's plain white T-shirt are rolled up so her tattoos show. The shirt and her jeans accentuate her breasts and hips and waist, a shape that too many men mistake as a license to stare or act stupid or worse. You have the body of a goddess, Francois said, more to himself than to her, through a flurry of kisses in this very spot the first time they had relieved each other of their clothes and conceded they were slaves to the depth of their passion. After childbirth and years of stress, gaining and losing weight and gaining it again, she hadn't felt like a goddess—just another tired woman in the city until she saw herself through the lens of his desire. Francois Avram Chevalson. Tall and lean as a swimmer, though a stranger to the ocean that surrounds his island home. Even now in the same pressed slacks and white shirt he wore in the morning to court. His long salt-and-pepper hair still tied in a ponytail. Francois who makes her feel beautiful even on the days she hates her pale skin and thinks her lips are too pink and thin. Francois with his deep-set green eyes that change color in the sun and indicate his capacity for lust that she knows only see her, no matter what other woman, rock star or refugee, is present.

"Oh look there's one," Francois says and she yearns to feel his close-clipped beard on her neck.

One of the creatures they call a bat, a thing more like a mad cross between a bird and a firefly, spirals from the seaside caves into the coming night. Foot-long, black wings extend to catch the wind and the "bat" bursts into golden flames. The bio-luminescent halo of light does not consume it as it glides leaving a glowing trail of its path through the sky that lingers.

"Why do they do it?" Michaela says.

"I don't know. It must feel right. Small brains. Bad eyes. They don't navigate by sight or reason."

"Is that true?"

Francois is one of the smartest people she knows and expert on monsters. But also expert on making things up. Even when he doesn't think he is.

"Think so," he says.

"Sure you're not projecting on it?"

Francois shrugs. Michaela realizes maybe she's the one projecting. "Feeling right" was how she'd navigated her way to him. When she had first seen his photo in the newspaper she didn't even think he was handsome. Intriguing, yes. What sort of a man represents monsters, she wondered. Her feelings drew her, but weariness of cruel city life and its drama was what kept her, that and the warrant for her arrest waiting back in the city. She had to lie low somewhere. Why not with him? At a time she cannot pinpoint, lust and convenience and intrigue turned to love. Painful, all-consuming, all-encompassing, inconvenient love.

They had met at a gallery show one of Rockstar's protégés was curating. Michaela was there looking for money. Looking for help. Francois was dragged there with a client, a handsome devil, who introduced them then disappeared into the debauchery going on in the buying room in the back. She was fascinated how this man could have the name Francois yet not speak a word of French. He was fascinated by how she had no plans to show up for her court date. But he didn't judge. He was interested. Even a little turned on by her troubles. A lot turned on but he didn't act on it. Not then. He called her the next afternoon and brought her groceries and was kind. He informed her about police methods and taught her how to be careful. For her birthday he took her to the Coney Island aquarium and they held hands, safe from the July sun and the pressures of their lives in that tourist refuge, watching tropical fish circle round and round.

The first time she traveled to Francois's property, the warrant for missing her court dates had been issued. She worried the police would pick her up at the ferry terminal. Francois reassured her that it was too soon for that but admonished her to "take care of her business before it took care of her," which struck her as an unromantic thing to say but didn't lessen her desire to see him and to take a break from her life—to spend time with the intriguing, kind stranger who was obviously so very hot for her and trying his best not to show it.

As he was showing her around she was most drawn to the guest house that overlooked the cliffs. He went to great pains to avoid letting her near, at first. The guest house was where his ex-wife had stayed during their split. All her things and clothes were left behind and he hadn't cleaned the place out nor ventured in since she had left. Michaela found this equally strange and exciting. After dinner that night they sat on the cliffs. The bats were out, filling the sky with golden fire.

Despite the rare display they could do nothing else but breathe into each other, unable to keep their lips apart even as they undressed. His skin on hers was charged with the excitement and comfort of remembering something lost in a dream, something vital yet somehow its absence had been forgotten.

"You know Rockstar called," Michaela says, unable to stop thinking of the heat of that first night.

"Oh? What'd she say?"

"She's doing a gallery show soon. In the city. A good job's waiting if I just say the word."

"Good. You should do it. I know you're the best and so does she."

"I'm not going to. You know why?"

"I know what you're going to say—"

"Why won't you fucking just help me?" Michaela says.

"How many times do I have to tell you?" Francois says. "I'm helping you by not helping you."

"It would be so easy for you. I don't believe any part of your twisted theory."

"It's not my theory. And it's not a theory. It just is. If you don't take care of things you got yourself into, yourself, the same sort of things are going to keep coming at you, only stronger and stronger until you learn what you are meant to."

"Why is it so important to you to teach me a lesson?" Michaela says. "Why don't you just love me?"

"I'm not teaching you anything. I'm not even certain what the lesson is. But I know for sure that you are meant to take care of the trouble you got yourself into and the lesson is in doing that. If you continue to ignore it—"

"Fuck you. If you really loved me, the way I love you, you wouldn't let me suffer."

"Are you suffering?" Francois says. "I'm not interfering in this because I do love you, why don't you see that?"

"Interfering? Is that what you think? No. No. No. I would do anything for you."

"I would do anything for you," Francois says.

"Except help me."

"I am helping you. If you keep ignoring the knocking at the door the universe is going to break the door down. It's the natural order of things. This is your wake up call. Take care of it or it's going to take care of you."

"You help monsters all day long. But not me. For me you have this gibberish."

"You aren't listening to a word I'm saying, are you?"

"I'm asking you to represent me in court. Help me fix a mistake I made so I can get on with my life and you're saying no. What is it I'm not hearing?"

The first night she had asked for his help she was lying in her bed in the guest house. He said she could stay there until she got strong again. Until she found her way, while she was taking care of her business. It made perfect sense at the time. She lay in bed that night watching for the bats but they never came. Every night since, she lies there watching for them through the window. Sometimes she sees them in her dreams. If he loved me, the way I love him, he would do anything, she thinks. Why doesn't he understand? If only he would just understand.

"I love you," Michaela says.

"I love you too."

He stands and walks behind her chair and drapes his arms around her. Her body comes alive with chills as his hands find her waist. She stands, knocks the chair down and presses against him.

"I want you. Now," she whispers, then bites his ear.

Together, embraced like this, they both believe that nothing is wrong. At least nothing that can't be overcome.

"Come inside with me," Francois says.

"No, come with me to the beach. I want you down there. On

the sand."

"It will be the death of us," he says.

"If it is, then that's how I want to go. Turned to stone. With you inside me."

They undress each other, reaching for the passion of that first night. She tries to drag him to the path to the beach, then succumbs to desire, pushes him down and mounts him. For a few minutes, before the mask of physical ecstasy wears off, they believe everything is indeed okay, and their troubles can be overcome.

On his morning walk before work, Francois finds his old neighbor Mrs. Grant on her side of the rock wall that divides their properties, watering her flower garden as she often is at this time of day.

"The girl still here?" she says.

"She has a name."

Mrs. Grant goes back to watering as if it requires the utmost concentration. Her wiry hands grasp her copper watering can and she blows wisps of her stringy gray hair out of her face. She doesn't comment on the hot morning sun or his growing moonflower vines or even the young basilisk sunning itself on the rock wall a dozen yards away. So Francois knows she's cross with him.

The lizard cranes its head up, red and orange skin catching the light in bright contrast to the patches of mottled black on its back.

"Out with it, Mrs. G," he says.

"You're being reckless," she blurts, not missing a beat after his cue. "Again."

"Reckless?"

"She's using you?"

"For what?"

"For shelter from her storms," she says.

"Isn't that what love is?" Francois says. "At least part of it?"

The young basilisk crawls along the wall. Its claws scrape on stone.

"Could be. But not for her," Mrs. G says. "This one, when she's strong enough to fly, she flies away from you."

"And how did you come up with this?"

"It's written all over her. All over both of you. You don't find it curious how the girl's problems perfectly match your professional expertise?"

"What's so curious about it? She wants me to represent her in court and take care of a mess she made."

"See, I told you."

"But I'm not. She got herself into it, she has to learn to get herself out of it. It's not about the money or my time. I wish it was that easy. She'll find her lessons in cleaning up the mess. Herself."

"Her? While *she* learns her lessons? The only lesson I see is for you."

"And what lesson does the universe have in store for me?"

"Such an adorable boy you are. Who said anything about the

universe? The universe has nothing to do with this. Or with anything. The only lessons are the ones we make up. The only meaning, to anything, is what we put there. I just hope you remember you've been used like this before."

"By who?"

"Claudine," she says.

"That was me," Francois says. "I didn't know what love was."

"You protest so quickly."

"How old was I? I didn't know how to give. To be selfless."

"That's how you see it?"

"I didn't know compassion, yet. Poor Claudine was caught in my wake."

"She was a sweet girl, that one, yes. I do believe she truly loved you. She would have waited for you to come around."

"She would have waited and waited. And crushed herself with the weight of years."

"And what about Esamae?"

"What about her?"

"You really don't see what I'm saying? You took her in, too. And as soon as she became strong enough, she left you."

"I haven't taken Michaela in."

"You haven't?"

"She's just staying here while she learns to take care of things."

"Just like Esamae."

"No. That was...something else. It wasn't personal."

"It wasn't? Seemed personal to you. How long until you

stopped hurting?"

"That was the past and—"

"Go ahead, child. Tell me the past doesn't equal the future as you are so fond of doing. I know it doesn't. But do you? Remember what I taught you. Take care of your business. Resolve your issues or you face them again and again. This time it looks like your unresolved business is poised to really take care of you good."

"Might look like it from your side of the wall. But that's not what's happening here, Mrs. G."

"I hope so. I like you. You're a nice boy and you take care of people. I want you to take care of yourself."

"I'll be fine, Mrs. G. I *am* taking care of myself."

"Does the girl know about Esamae?"

"Why does my ex-wife matter?"

"She doesn't. I guess. Guess she matters so little there's no reason to tell the girl?"

Something metal clangs and there is a hiss, then the sound of something scraping against rock. The young basilisk has walked into one of Mrs. G's bear traps she has left on the wall. The steel-toothed manacle has clamped shut crushing the young creature's body. It rubs its head and tail on the rock as it dies.

"I wish you wouldn't do that, Mrs. G."

"They eat my flowers," she says.

"There are other ways."

"I know you think the young things are so pretty," she says. "But they grow up deadly. And faster than you think."

Michaela puts the goggles on and stares at the young basilisk chewing on Francois's morning glories. She makes sure the goggles are on securely even though she knows the young thing's gaze will not gain the ability to petrify for years to come.

She found the goggles in a hatbox in one of the storage sheds and just knew the box and its contents, two pairs of midnight lenses, belonged to Francois's ex-wife and what they were. Midnight lenses. What professionals use when dealing with phantasmagorical entities and creatures like basilisks. The best sex shops sell them too. They're worn when one wants to make love and not turn to stone. At least not fully. Or irreversibly. Francois is a sick fuck but his ex must have been even sicker, Michaela thinks and for the first time is jealous. She puts them back in the box and puts the box on the floor when she hears Francois is home and walking toward the back porch.

"Rockstar called again," Michaela says. "Invited me to a warehouse party."

"We should go," Francois says.

"No. That's not how it goes with her. She invited *me*."

"Then you should go."

"You think so?"

"Of course."

"You're not jealous?"

"I want you to do what you are meant to do," he says. "Being in their world. Around them. Going to their parties. Curating their shows is what you say you are meant to do and I agree. You have the eye for it. You're one of the best."

Michaela wants to tell him she loves him but instead says, "I only wish my court date was just taken care of."

"So why won't you?" he says.

"Why won't *you*?" she says. "Not tonight. I can't have this fight tonight."

"Why won't Rockstar or one of her protégés take care of it if they need you to work and want you around?"

"That's not how it's done," Michaela says.

"Exactly. This is exactly what I've been saying all along. That's not how it's done. You need to take care of this. In all the details you'll find the—"

"Lesson, right? Lessons again. What is this big lesson that I'm missing that's so important to you?"

"I don't know. But you do. You will."

"I go back to the city I could go to jail. Is that part of my lesson?"

"Maybe," Francois says.

"You'd let me go to jail?"

"Maybe."

"That's a change. I thought you'd say 'of course.' Maybe you love me after all."

"I'd miss you in jail."

"Such a romantic, my man. Even when you're being incorrigible," she says and kisses him.

She can't bear the feeling of his lips and beard on her neck and tugs his shirt out of his slacks. They free themselves of their clothes, their only thoughts being breath into breath, the thoughtlessness of passion fueled by each other's touch. Michaela backs up, off the porch leading him down the stairs onto the lawn without breaking their kiss.

"Come on now, at the beach," she says.

"What?"

"Take me. On the beach."

"Down there? We'll turn to stone."

"I have the lenses."

"What?"

"From the box in the shed."

For a second she thinks he will stop kissing her. Stop touching her and react with outrage. Or questions. Or just stop. When he does none of these things she asks again.

"I really want to," she says.

She doesn't care about the danger. When they are kissing like this there is nothing else. All the pain. All the unfairness. All the loss are just things. Things outside her that no longer have to be dealt with. Things that no longer have to be overcome. Sometimes she thinks her life is already over. That it ended on the day everything happened. To spend forever without pain. Without care. Even the temptation of such a fate is the biggest rush she can imagine.

"The lenses will only slow it," he says. "We'll turn to stone."

"Don't you want to feel yourself turn to stone? Inside me? Kissing me, like this. Forever in this moment?"

"No," Francois says and pulls her on top of him.

For a second she thinks of fighting the pleasure. Of fighting him. Then leading him, luring him, teasing him down to the beach. But with a shudder, her logical thought recedes to bliss and she is tired of fighting.

Michaela is up early to see Francois off to the ferry for work. Court actually starts on time in the summer so Francois does not have the luxury to walk the rock wall and chat with Mrs. G as he would like. Michaela has convinced him to go to Rockstar's party in her place. She said if he went he would understand her, and everything she'd been asking and he could not refuse. They've decided to move her into the house over the weekend. Another grown basilisk made the climb and almost surprised Michaela. The main house will be safer. Farther from the cliffs. In the house they will be together but Mrs. G's words echo in his mind.

Rockstar's warehouse is across from the docks in the seaport, not far from where Francois catches the ferry. Francois figures he will go for an hour and still have time to catch the last ferry home. He thinks about Esamae. One day she stopped being herself. Life and the pretty illusions she and he and the world had created were no longer good enough for her. She felt compelled to leave him, to sail into the darkness in order to continue being her. And it didn't matter to her if she ever came back or if he or their life would be there if she did. Mrs. G thought she knew it all, but didn't understand it wasn't that Esamae didn't love him. She couldn't. She was no longer meant for this world anymore, she was no longer a part of it and had to go, go to a place he could not and would not follow. That's just the way things go sometimes, he thinks. The thought is the product of a lot of painful reasoning and the distance of time. He doesn't want to be without Michaela but he knows if she wants to throw her life away there is nothing he can do to stop her, even if he tries. Mrs. G just doesn't understand that.

Rockstar's people are waiting for him at the door to the warehouse. His name is on their list. The bouncer, a tall thin woman with short gray hair, wears a silk black dress that reminds him of one Esamae used to always wear. Esamae had always wanted to go down to the beach. On the last night he ever saw her, she did. He wonders if she is still down there. On the sand. With the basilisks. Her last expression of rage, of indifference, frozen forever in stone. Or if she just finally left like she had been threatening to do and went to the shores beneath the cliffs and sailed away. He's never checked. At first because of fear, then later on indifference. Whatever her fate, it no longer matters, he tells himself.

"You okay, Mister—"

"Chevalson," Francois says.

The bouncer hands him a black handkerchief and motions to his eyes. Has he been crying?

She leads him inside. The ceilings are three stories high. In some places wooden crates, some large enough to hold elephants or full wall paintings, are stacked to the top.

A few dozen people have gathered in an empty space between the massive rows of crates about fifty yards away. Seven or eight paintings on easels ring the boundary of their makeshift party space. The group's clothing styles are an eclectic cross section of what one sees in the city. One bunch are wearing evening wear suited for a night at the opera. Another are dressed in business attire like Francois. A few others flitting about from group to group are clad in jeans and leather and worn black boots, despite the summer heat outside. One woman is the center of gravity of all their orbits. Michaela's Rockstar.

Rockstar watches Francois approach, ignoring the chatter of those around her and says, "Michaela's beau," as soon as he is in ear shot.

The people around her fawn over him when introduced. They exchange pleasantries. Small talk. Complaints about the weather. They coo over Michaela's beauty and profess to miss her. They coo over his job and recent photograph in the newspaper. He recognizes them as sycophants but Rockstar is different. She allows them all to spin around her. She feigns to be a diva but Francois knows she is listening. Taking it all in yet ignoring it at the same time. She's taking him in and sizing him up.

"Let me show Mister Francois my paintings," she says.

The crowd shifts so Francois can see the one displayed on the nearest easel. It is abstract and reminds him of the red-orange and black mottled pattern of young basilisk skin.

"Not these ones," she says and leads him out of the crowd to an avenue between two massive skyscrapers of crates. "This way, dear," she says.

As she leads him through a maze of turns she coos over Michaela. Her talent. Her eye for good art. Her beauty. He wonders if they have been lovers.

Rockstar stops and adjusts her white button-up shirt. Too many buttons are undone and Francois spies what he thinks is bright green ink in the center of her flat chest. Then he sees the leaves and thorns. Heartvine.

Rockstar scratches at the plant symbiotically bonded to her body.

"Congratulations," Francois says. "I didn't peg you for the monogamous type."

"There is nothing else but love," she says. "No higher purpose. All this. It's pretty. It's fun. It pays the bills. But it is show. Surely you see that. Surely you know that. I was so happy when I heard sweet lost Michaela landed someone like you. I can tell. You love her. You are good for her."

"How can you know?"

"I do. I have an eye for these things. You don't get to where I am without seeing things as they are and acting accordingly. The one question I have is why you haven't yet taken care of her court dates, Mister Francois?"

"Why don't you?"

"Why it's her business," Rockstar says. "She's meant to take care of it. If she doesn't it will only come back to bite her ten times over. I can't have any of that kind around me. What we don't take care of takes care of us, you know?"

"I think I know what you mean," he says. But he is not pleased to hear words he has said so often from her. They feel predatory the way she speaks them and it has triggered something defensive inside him.

"She really loves working for you," Francois says. "And she's the best at what she does."

"I know that, darling. You wouldn't be here giving me an update on her if she wasn't. But most of all I love her for her mean right hook."

"Her what?"

"Her mean right hook. The girl knows how to throw quite the punch. Oh. She hasn't told you?"

"Told me what?"

"About her warrant?"

"I know about that. She was taken in with everyone in that big bar fight."

"She wasn't just taken in. She started it. Best fight I ever saw. In a bar or otherwise. Two monsters, absolute thugs, wouldn't leave me alone. Your lover girl got all up in them. She's very protective."

"Michaela started all that? I just don't see it."

"On any given day I'm with you. But she was out for the first time since she'd put her son in the ground."

"Her son?"

"A mother shouldn't have to ever bury her child. Especially when they're killed by a monster like the ones you represent day in and day out. How much do you charge to represent someone who's killed because they've had too much to drink behind the wheel?"

"I didn't know."

"I see that. Now you see why she started a fight. And hit one of the creeps so hard he fell. Fell and hit his head just right that he cracked his skull."

"I didn't know the charge she was running from was so serious. And that—"

"Now you know. Wonder why she never told you."

Rockstar rambles on but Francois is barely listening. It takes all of his composure to not break into a run. She's a monster who only cares for Michaela so long as she is useful to her. It dawns on him he was wrong to think of sending her back to them and their shallow world. He was wrong to let her find her own way out of the mess. It wasn't that she wasn't capable. She just needed help. Help being ready to deal. And not having to face it alone.

He excuses himself to go to the restroom and exits the warehouse. He is going home to Michaela. He's going to move her into the house and he is going to tell her he was wrong. Monday morning he is going to arrange to have her case taken care of.

On the way to the ferry he stops and picks up a bunch of red roses at the first flower stand he passes. Sitting on the ferry he has a better idea. When it docks he leaves the roses behind and stops at the merchant who sold him his flower beds and purchases a heartvine bulb. Much better than roses.

Michaela is waiting for him on the front porch and she is holding a heartvine bulb, too. She's had the same idea and has purchased one, too. Once planted the vines grow together, binding the host planters. Changing them. Joining them. Irrevocably. There is no divorce after heartvine. No cutting the roots out. You are bonded forever. Heartvine flowers bloom once a year and only the host couple can see the bloom of their plant.

They kiss. Michaela leads him outside. As they are tearing off each other's clothes she grabs the goggles from the box on the patio. She leads him past the lawn to the winding stairs, hewn from the jagged stone cliff, that descend to the beach. They make love on the sand as giant lizards crawl back and forth past them. When the lizards look upon him Francois feels his body wanting to change. Wanting to turn to stone. The lenses are working but the feeling is not like he expected. He hadn't expected...pleasure. More basilisks come. And ignore them as they traverse the sand to the rocks jutting into the water and eat the dark-green algae. Michaela wonders if this is the reason they are here. The algae. Maybe there is nothing mystic about why they are here at all. She climbs on top of Francois and takes him again. The bats are out and fill the sky with fire. Michaela takes it as a sign. A sign never to lose him. To get her shit together. To take care of her court case, herself. Somehow, everything is going to be okay. She celebrates by teasing Francois; pulling on his goggles.

"Don't you want to turn to stone? Don't you want to turn to stone," she says.

"Whatever you want," he says. "Anything for you."

Later as they are lying there on their backs in the sand watching the bats, a big basilisk returns from the rocks. Its tail dragging in the sand makes a hissing sound as it passes.

"How was the party?" Michaela asks.

"I've changed my mind. I'm taking care of your case. Monday we're going to court."

Michaela holds his hand tighter as the sky fills with fire.

On Monday morning they take the ferry to the city together. The plan is for Michaela to meet Rockstar at one of her galleries, then after lunch come to court to meet Francois after he has arranged for a lawyer for her. One of his colleagues. It is too personal for him to handle himself. He's too close to it. Then they are going to go home to continue moving and to get ready to plant their vines.

Michaela is late for court. Francois delays the proceeding and waits in the hall watching his phone.

At 3 p.m. she texts him. "I'm with Rockstar. One of her friends' beach house up the coast. An impromptu party."

"A party? Now?" he texts. "I've set everything up. You are due in court."

"Take care of it. Please. I have to do this."

"You have to do this," he texts.

He can't believe he is having this fight with her. Again. Here. Now. Via text.

"You told me I was the best and I'm meant to do this," she texts. "So I'm doing it."

"I didn't mean you should throw everything away by going for it now."

"You believing in me meant so much to me. Don't take that away."

"Do you want to go to jail? Do you want to remain a fugitive forever? I'm doing what you wanted me to do and you're just running away."

Francois does not hear from her the rest of the day. Nor the rest of the evening. Or night.

The next morning he does not check on the heartvines they have carefully wrapped in fertilized wet towels for planting. He goes to the rock wall.

When Mrs. G sees him coming she says something sarcastic and challenging to him, then ceases when she sees his face.

"You poor boy," she says. "You can't love someone who is hell bent on self-destruction. You can't. No one can."

"You were right," he says. "You tried to warn me."

"I hate it," she says. "I hate to see you like this."

"I don't understand," he says. "I guess it doesn't matter anymore if I do."

Francois takes out his phone.

"Do not come back," Francois texts to Michaela.

There is no reply.

"Never come back," he adds.

Then he steels himself to go to work.

Two days later Michaela texts him.

"You gave me a gift. The gift of your belief in me. Belief that I was the best. You helped show me what I was meant to do. Why does it feel like you are taking that back?"

Francois does not reply. He makes it through the work week without replying, though he often wants to. On Saturday he closes up his house and gives Mrs. G the keys.

"Where are you going?" she asks.

"Don't know," he says. "Take care of the place while I'm gone taking care of myself."

"Of course," she says. "It will be here when you get back."

Francois is lucky that he has worked hard in his life. He has enough wealth that he never has to go home again. He travels to places where no one knows his name. Places where no one will remember him. In the second month of his travels he finds himself in a fancy bar next to a very expensive hotel on the shore of a Caribbean Island.

A young woman sits next to him. For the first time in months he engages in real conversation. For the first time in months he does not think of Michaela. After a half hour of talking he realizes how much fun he is having. The woman is smart and carefree. He notices his chest no longer feels tight.

The conversation turns to his home. He told her he used to live near basilisk cliffs. She says she's always wanted to go. A drunk woman, who had been listening, jumps in to their conversation.

"Tell me," the drunk woman says. "How do you make love and not turn to stone?"

Seeing his reaction the first woman apologizes for the question.

The tension in his chest returns. For a moment when the woman's attention was on him, he had forgotten Michaela.

Dusk's last light is almost gone and the sky's evening blues are darkening in a way that he and Michaela used to find so beautiful.

A man with a wet suit half on, half off, comes up from the beach and throws his arms around the woman Francois has been talking to and kisses her.

"You can't," Francois answers.

"Can't what?" the woman's husband says.

"Doesn't matter," Francois says.

He doesn't listen to their chatter. It doesn't matter. He doesn't like the disdain and pity he hears in their voices. Maybe someday he'll know love again, love like theirs. Maybe someday he'll be in a place like this and not be alone. Maybe someday he'll return to Mrs. G and ask for the key to his place back.

A bat spirals into the almost-night sky. It leaves behind a golden trail of flame that does not consume it.

DANIEL BRAUM

AN AMERICAN GHOST IN ZURICH

1. Coalesce

Mom and Dad are walking me to the gate, and I can't help but think of Jaz. After all these years, what would he think?

"I can't wait to learn what the project is," Dad says.

"I probably won't ever be able to tell you," I say.

"I know. I'm just so proud they're flying my girl, the scientist, to Zurich," Dad says a bit too loud.

"She's a grown woman. Don't embarrass her, dear," Mom says.

"Particle physicist, Dad. Say it. Par-ti-cal."

"You may be a VP and a PhD but you'll always be my little VIP," Dad says.

Jaz would be critical. Of Dad's corny jokes. Of me. Of

everything. Like he was before I left him. He'd have a reason why this assignment is a waste of my talents. I can almost hear him going on about why my education was beneath me. As was my grant. My research. Even the project at the neutrino collector.

I sigh and blow my bangs out of my eyes. This was where we said goodbye. Where I saw him off to Europe. That moment is so far away, and I hate that it still haunts me. I feel the weight of the years, of the silence, of the...nothing. He and I are just nothing. Like two electrons without covalent bonds, hurtling through this world, never to share orbits again. Even if we weren't meant to be together, we could have at least been more than that.

Mom and Dad are bickering. Something or another about me. As usual. I slip my earbuds in. With the sound of School of Seven Bells I come alive. Everything is a black-and-white movie, and I'm a streak of color moving through the frames. Ethereal harmonies wash over me. Beautiful, but not quite on. Imperfect. Just like our fractured universe and everything in it.

A photo appears on my phone. Pria and I at my send-off party. My finger is pointing down my throat to show what I thought of the music my students had playing.

Pria doesn't see music as a way to transcend. To her, it's just to reinforce the shiny, happy place she lives in. I love her anyway.

Bon Voyage, she texts.

I'm so excited, I text back. *I'm thinking of dying my hair pink.*

But what would the Aeon-Hartlin board think?

I know, I text.

Plus, Dad would die. My degrees still hang in my old room with my grade-school science fair ribbons. To him I'll always be a little girl. I'm some kind of outsider to everyone else. Here I am thinking of Jaz like I don't want to be, but even at the end, with all the bad, when I was with him I always felt like a woman.

Mom's voice intrudes, out of time from the beat.

"...I know but I still think we should tell her, dear."

"Quiet, she'll hear. No good can come of it," Dad says.

"Tell me what?" I ask.

"See, now you've done it," Dad says.

"Out with it," I say. "My plane leaves in less than an hour. Then I'm going to be busy with the project for who knows how long, so now or never."

"I hate it that they won't tell you what you're working on," Mom says. "It's probably dangerous."

"Don't change the subject, Mom."

She sighs.

"It's Jaz, honey," she says.

"What?!"

"He called while you were in the shower this morning," she says.

"Jaz? How come you didn't—"

"He didn't sound...right, dear. I didn't want to upset you."

"Mother. Tell."

"Now you've done it," Dad says.

"He had a message for you," Mom says. "Told you not to

come."

"No," Dad says. "You're confused. He said the message was *to* come."

"Dear, I distinctly heard him say *not* to come."

"Jaz. I can't believe it," I say. "All these years. Figures he picks today to send me a message."

"Thing is, he said the message wasn't from him," Mom says. "He said the message was from you."

"From me?"

"That part's right," Dad says. "He said *you* told him to tell you."

"That's impossible," I say. "I haven't seen him in, what, nine years? I've never even been to Zurich, if that's where he still is."

"Apparently so," Mom says.

"I told you this would only upset her," Dad says.

"I'm not upset. I don't care. He's nuts."

I hear myself say the words but I don't believe them. He was brilliant. At least once upon a time he was.

"See? I told you it wouldn't be a problem," Mom says.

"Good. Come on then," Dad says. "There's just enough time to have a coffee with my favorite particle physicist."

I ease back into the first-class seat Aeon provided. The plane takes to the air and I slip my earbuds in, even though devices aren't permitted yet. The stale cabin atmosphere is replaced by the Seven Bells' electronic beats. Lush, open guitar chords join in one at a time. With each layer the song swells. It is more than a song. It is an emotional reality. A story. A truth. The passion is so real I feel that the woman in the song who lost her heart could be me.

The plane hits cruising altitude and the seatbelt sign turns off. I'm thinking about the death of the guitar player and falling asleep to their refrains.

In my dreams I hear Seven Bells songs I have never heard before. They are strange and wonderful and I hope I remember them when I wake.

"Wake up. Stop dreaming," says a familiar voice.

I open my eyes. Someone is right there, standing over me. The plane lurches. The lights go out. Dim emergency lights flicker on. The person is gone. A flight attendant rushes through the aisle to the coach cabin. I look around for who woke me and realize I don't recognize the song that is playing. My player lists five Seven Bells albums, but they made only three. I don't recognize the song titles. My phone dies. An uneasy murmur fills the cabin. I wonder if I am still asleep, but it doesn't feel like it. The canned air and the harsh perfume of the woman next to me are too real. Static replaces the murmur and my phone powers back up. The strange albums and songs are gone. Did I dream them? No. Coffee has made my breath stale in the most un-dreamlike way.

The cabin lights return.

"Wow, bumpy ride," says the man sitting across the aisle.

As I hit PLAY to start the song again, two flight attendants and a woman enter the cabin from coach.

"Yeah, that's her," the woman says.

"Ma'am, I can confirm this woman has been here in her seat the entire time," says the flight attendant nearest me. His name, Oliver, is spelled out in cursive orange letters on his jacket. His face is kind. I like the dapper way he has put himself together.

"No. That's her," the woman says.

"Ma'am, you'll have to take your seat," the other attendant says and leads the woman away.

"I'm sorry," Oliver says to me. "We had an unruly passenger after we hit that turbulence. That woman said she saw you while boarding and was convinced the unruly passenger was you. On behalf of the airline I'd like to apologize."

Was the unruly passenger in here? I try to recall her but she was only a shape in the dark.

The man across the aisle is chatting at me but I'm not listening. I'm too drained to tell him to stop. From what few words I do say, he thinks I'm traveling to do some sort of engineering work on the CERN particle collider in Geneva.

He drones on. The woman's voice is so familiar but I can't place it. It eludes me like the name of a song on the tip of my tongue.

2. Converge

Luggage circulates on the carousel. As I watch for my bag, I try to remember the songs I heard during the disturbance. Someone taps me on the shoulder. It's Oliver.

"This is for you," he says, and he hands me a crumpled piece of paper.

"What?" I fumble to unfold the paper.

"No. Not here. Shhhh...," he whispers. "It's from you. You said you'd know. Or you would know."

What's with everyone? I only want to get to the hotel, close the door and leave this day outside.

He attempts to act nonchalant by checking his phone and pretending to watch the carousel while furtively glancing at me. After a moment, he nods to me then walks away. I unfold the paper. On it are hand-drawn sketches of machine parts. Long strings of numbers. Formulas.

I crumple the paper and look for a trashcan. As my bag arrives, I stick the paper in my pocket.

My hotel is in a beautiful square in Old Town, near the river. The cobblestone street does not permit vehicles, so my escort from Aeon carries my bags from the carpark. There is a music store with violins in the window. A liquor shop displays bottles of spirits I have never heard of. People are drinking coffee at tables outside cafes. There is a world of rooftop gardens atop the four- and five-story buildings flanking the narrow road. This is everything I imagined Europe to be. At the hotel, my escort gestures for the bellboy to take my bags.

"Ms. Hartlin wishes to see you right away," he says.

Aeon-Hartlin is headquartered outside the city in a low-rise building of metal and glass centered on sprawling, manicured grounds. Pines and large gray stones and rugged mountains in the distance are reflected in the polished surfaces. With all the angles and curves, and the glare of the afternoon sun, it is hard to discern the building's exact shape.

The receptionist takes my photo as I sign in. My face is on the printed paper pass he directs me to wear. Floor-to-ceiling octagonal windows span the large lobby. We exit through double doors opposite the entrance and emerge into a giant office. The dozens of people at desks and phone banks barely give us notice. My escort punches a code into a keypad at another set of doors and we enter a production area. Conveyor belts transport metal parts while automated mechanical arms work on them.

We pass sterile booths, spray-coating areas, and more guarded checkpoints. I know it is a show. Finally we enter a large conference room where dozens of my colleagues and rivals are seated at a big, polished metal table. I'm seated next to Wendy Mikaela, a chemist I used to know. I last heard she was working for a Pfizer subsidiary. Wendy lifts her glass to me in greeting. My escort asks me if I want anything and then joins the other attendants waiting along the perimeter of the room. A minute later, Rudolph Cellantino, a metallurgist whose work I recently read about, is escorted to the last empty space at the table next to me. The attendants exit, leaving the door near the head of the table open.

Ilsa Hartlin walks in. She's much taller than I pictured. I know her only as a photograph and a reproduced signature on my pay bonuses. Her thin, gray hair is neatly pulled back.

"I want to thank you all for coming," she says. "Before our work begins, I must tell you the reason you are here is not what we told you. I apologize to those who were told nothing. We did what we had to do to bring you here. Look around. This is the greatest gathering of minds we could assemble. The task before us holds great challenges, challenges worthy of you. But it will force us into an area of moral uncertainty. I regret I can tell you no more at the moment. Yet, with this, you must decide whether to proceed. If you wish to leave we hope you will remain in Zurich as our guest until you return home. You will be generously compensated for your time."

A woman I'm pretty sure is Shaenna Vanderhousen, an aeronautical engineer working for Japan's private sector, stands up. Her shoes echo on the white marble floor as she exits. Wendy Mikaela finishes her drink and looks to me and Rudolph with an innocent grin.

"I'm in. Are you?" she asks.

"I'm certainly intrigued," Rudolph says.

I'm intrigued too. The entrance door opens and the black-clad attendants wheel in serving carts, and the aroma of hot chocolate fills the space. Steaming mugs and simple white plates with small octagons of chocolate are served to us. Ilsa Hartlin looks angry, then confused. She whispers something to an attendant, then smiles.

"Aeon-Hartlin wants you to stay," she says. "All of you. Before we can proceed we require your solemn pledge of secrecy. The required documents are coming shortly. Please rest and enjoy yourselves tonight. Tomorrow we need the best you have."

I stand with the group and find myself walking with Wendy and Rudolph.

"We're all going out for authentic Swiss food and then drinks," Wendy says. "God help me if I know what that is, but you want to come?"

I do. Even though I'm dead tired.

Zurich at night is beautiful. The stone streets. The river. The sounds of gathered people chase away the silence of age and night. Wendy, Rudolph, and a half dozen others from the room stroll through the streets of the square near my hotel. Shopkeepers are closing their doors. Restaurants are lighting candles and preparing outdoor tables. Rudolph and Wendy choose a restaurant on crowded Niederdorfstrasse. I eat steak tartar. And things I don't recognize. I drink the wine Wendy pours. There is chocolate. And laughter. Nobody talks about inane music or American TV. These people are brilliant, and it feels like being in school before I met

Jaz.

After dinner, we wander through the streets and across the footbridge leading out of Old Town.

"I didn't know there was a red-light district." Wendy says. "What fun."

She's had too much to drink. So have I.

Not all of the girls in the windows have sad eyes. Some are just strange, some are just empty. Rudolph and Wendy and the others are loving it and discussing which brothel bar we will go to, as if they are picking dinner. For a moment, I think I am okay with it. But I'm not. I go back to the bridge, back to the square to find my hotel. The square is crowded with people drinking and singing. The whole mob is singing a theme song from some popular cartoon. Jaz would know. He would mock them. I smile.

Jasper Rodrigo Van Houton. Son of a geologist from Mexico City and a Dutch archaeologist. Named after his parents' favorite stone. The bright-eyed young man I met in a man-made underground lake designed to capture proof of the elusive particles left over from the moment of creation. My neutrino collector project.

This is perfect water, he said. *Perfect like you. You're like a neutrino. Unnoticed, hell even undetectable by most everyone. The indifference and cruelty of people don't stop you. They are unable to grasp the perfection that is you even when you're right under their noses.* He meant it. And he hadn't been drunk like the fools tonight. He hadn't cared how he sounded or that he didn't quite make sense. It was the nicest thing anyone had said to me, ever.

The memory makes all the awful things he said later hurt that much more.

I didn't love him for saying that. I loved him for singing to me. The first song was about the universe and a cosmic star-crossed love. Another was about everything being in its perfect place and time. Learning there was more to him than his scientist's mind was like finding an undiscovered property of one of my favorite elements.

The songs were pieces of him. Cherished, fragile, secret pieces of him, and he found me worthy of them. Through them he exposed his authentic self to me. Giving them to me, he gave himself to me. I didn't care about his scarred lip. Or his funny eye, or his hair that wouldn't stay combed, or his spindly arms and legs. The way he looked at me and the way he treated me, back then, was beautiful. When I was with him the world didn't feel broken.

Finding him on social media is easier than I expected. I call.

"Anina Washington," he says. "Thank goodness."

"You're not the type to keep an online profile," I say.

"I know," he says. "I put the account up for you."

He gives me directions. His flat is in Old Town, above a clock shop. I don't recognize him when he greets me at the building's door. His hair is long and in a ponytail. His face is lined and shows the wear of years of drinking.

"You called my parents," I say. "Don't ever do that again."

"I won't," he says. "You're unlisted. Your office wouldn't put my calls through. Will you come in?" he asks.

"No. I don't want to."

"Then how about we go to the garden?"

I follow him up four flights of stairs to the roof. Potted plants fill almost every inch of space. There is a little iron table and two small chars. Absinthe and beer bottles are neatly lined around the pots, each an untold story, each a relic of a night since I last saw him.

"What's so important?" I ask.

"You tell me," he says. "Why contact me after all these years?"

"I did no such thing."

"You did. Last week, at my parents' anniversary in Barcelona."

"No, I didn't."

"You were older and grayer but you were you," he says.

He looks at me like I am an unsolved equation.

"Yes. It was you. And you told me to call you yesterday with the message."

"And you believed this person? You've been drinking."

"Yes, I have. Very much. But she knew where to come. She knew about the neutrino collector."

"All right, that's odd," I say. "But it doesn't prove anything."

"I'm supposed to stop you from working on something," he says. "A great machine."

"I don't even know what that is."

"You were supposed to have a piece of paper for me. To show you."

"Well, I don't."

"No?" he says, and covers his face with his hands. "She—I was certain you would."

I don't like how upset he is. The Jaz I remembered wasn't this...gullible.

"What's going on?" he asks. "These people. These...yous. They've been haunting me. Are you just another one of them?"

"No, I'm me."

I reach for his hand to comfort him and somehow we are embracing. The side of my face touches his. The stubble on his face is soft. He smells like strong alcohol and something unnameable I'd forgotten until now. If I turn my head our lips will meet.

"No, I can't do this," I say.

"Do what?"

"This."

"What? I thought I'd never see you again until you showed up. I'm not asking for anything. I just don't want to be haunted anymore."

"Haunted? What the hell is a ghost anyway?" I yell.

I brace myself for him to yell back. For him to launch into one of his long convoluted tirades. There's only fear and resignation on his face.

"I don't know. Just help me, please. Okay? If anyone can figure this out, you can."

3. Axis. The Machine

"There are fewer of you here today than I had hoped for," Ilsa Hartlin says.

Only Wendy, Rudolph, and I and three others have returned to the conference room. Ilsa Hartlin takes us through the door at the head of the conference table.

"I'm glad you're here," Ilsa says to me.

I find it strange that I'm singled out.

No guards or attendants accompany us. Ilsa leads us into an elevator that descends fast. We're going deep.

"You knew it was a collider," Wendy whispers to Rudolph.

Rudolph smiles.

The elevator opens into a cavernous space, the largest I have been in since the neutrino collector.

A giant machine towers over us, a monolithic rectangle as tall as my hotel, but wider. It is faintly luminous, giving off a soft glow that doubles our shadows.

Next to it is the track of a particle accelerator, a tunnel cut into the cavern's rock wall filled with rails, magnets, and metallic plating.

"Ha! I knew it," Rudolph says.

"On," Ilsa says.

Blue and white lights on the particle accelerator come to life. The tunnel extends as far as we can see in both directions—a high-tech subway line of electromagnetic fields generating energy to move particles together on collision courses, so their explosions can be monitored.

The great machine thrums. I imagine the sound is the music of the microcosmos, like the music of the spheres, only the perfect intervals are between vibrating particles, not planets. A six-by-six square of light appears in front of the machine. The square grows and an image appears on it. Water. Dark water. In another cavern.

"What is it?" Wendy asks. "A particle accelerator and a hologram?"

"Yes, that is an accelerator," Ilsa says. "Our track goes through Italy, Turkey, and Russia, among other places."

One of the other scientists gasps. "If that is true, it's larger than CERN. I can't imagine the cooperation needed to make that happen."

"We've been busy," Ilsa says.

"Working on a hologram?" Wendy says. "The resolution is astounding but—"

"It is not a picture," Ilsa says. "But the machine is a camera, of sorts. I think of it more as a window maker."

"Windows? To where?" I ask.

But I know where. It's the neutrino collector. The man-made lake under Illinois.

"Not where, when," she says. "We are looking into the past. Where? I'm not certain. I was hoping you could help."

"Time travel?" Wendy asks.

Rudolph scoffs.

"With enough energy, perhaps," Ilsa says. "This doesn't move matter. It opens windows and sends images. Like a camera."

"These images. Can they interact?" I ask.

"With enough energy I think they could," she says. "The amounts needed for that would be astounding."

I look at the accelerator track. She smiles.

"Ghosts," I say. "Interactive images from the past and future."

"You brought us here because you think this is a time travel machine?" Rudolph says.

"Aeon built this?" I ask, ignoring Rudolph.

"We had help," Ilsa says.

"Listen to me. This isn't funny," he says and storms toward the machine and walks right into the image square.

The collider's lights surge and an awful whir fills the cavern. All goes dark. The machine's thrumming hits a fever pitch then stops, the lights return. Rudolph has walked through the square. He walks a few more steps then turns around. His smile is gone. He looks at us like a lost child looking for a parent, then recognition blooms on his face.

"I don't want to be here," he says.

Ilsa helps him sit on the rough cavern floor.

"Rudolph, what happened?" she asks. "What did you see?"

For a second I think he will speak, but he only hangs his head and sobs.

"You knew that would happen," I say to her. "No guards here. No protection. It's happened before, hasn't it?"

"Please. Calm, please," she says. "I've brought you here for help."

"Help for what? Corporate profits?"

"Aeon-Hartlin is wildly profitable without this project," she says. "History shows us the genie cannot be put back in the bottle. The Manhattan Project. Look at what that brought us. *All of us.* Humankind. I seek your help, to help all of us. This transcends corporate interest. Nationality. I'm a CEO. A mother. A daughter. And so much more. But what happens with this is not for me to decide."

Ilsa looks around the cavern.

"Because I know this is something grand. We are on the verge of a breakthrough. What do you think? What do you see, Anina? Does it look familiar?"

"Of course it does," I say. "The neutrino detector. That's my life."

"I thought it might be," she says.

"Why?"

"I have my ideas, but I was hoping you'd tell me."

I bend down next to Rudolph.

"What did you see?" I ask.

His lips quiver, his eyes are red from tears.

"Let's all calm down and take him back to the elevator," Wendy says.

"No, that's my life over there," I say.

I run through the image square.

"Wait," Ilsa yells.

I hear her, but the sound is far away. I'm in the boat, with Jaz, checking the photo sensors in the neutrino collector. He is telling me how I'm like a neutrino. I can see them, countless thousands of dots of light, falling through the earth. Passing through the spaces between molecules. Passing through everything unnoticed until one is lucky enough to collide with a particle while our sensors are trained on it and we detect it. It is so beautiful. A shower of the most beautiful fireworks I have ever seen.

Everything begins to fade. The cavern. The boat. The water. Jaz. Only the shower of neutrinos remains. Then there is only blackness.

The dark isn't empty. I feel something. Presences. There are sounds. Like the sound of the machine and the accelerator but different, darker. Is this the sound of the darkness? Of dark matter? Is this the voice of the void? Voices of the things that inhabit it? Voices of things that do not coexist with light and the world we know? I don't feel malice, or evil. My instincts say these things here just are, same as we just are. And they are just doing what they do. There is a terrible sound. I think something sees me.

Ilsa is screaming. "Off! Off! Off!"

I'm back in the cavern with the great machine.

The accelerator powers down with a descending whir. The machine's pitch crescendos, then stops. I storm for the elevator.

"Don't go," Ilsa says. "We need you."

I hit UP.

"We need heroes," she calls as the door closes.

"You have all this," I scream. "Go find one."

4. Crumple. Diverge.

She said heroes, really? Pria texts.

Yeah, I text back.

Good one. I know you said you couldn't tell me what is really going on, but hey, great story.

Not a story, I text, and attach a selfie with my newly dyed pink hair.

Whoa. Didn't expect that. You okay?

Never better, I reply.

I drink my coffee and watch passersby on the cobblestone streets as I look over the crumpled paper the flight attendant gave me. Dad calls.

"Pria showed me the photo," Dad says. "Is that an absinthe bottle I see?"

"I'm fine, Dad. I love you."

"Well you've got your mother worried. She wants to talk to you."

There is quiet, then Mom is on the phone.

"I'm not worried," she says. "Your father loves the drama."

"Mom I—"

"Dear, I understand. You explained everything."

"I did?"

"You came here," she says. "One of you did. I understand. And I agree. You never asked to be born. Neither did I. 'This universe is made up of elements blown apart from one cosmic whole at the Big Bang, the moment of creation,' you said."

"The fractured universe," I say.

"Yes, that's how you put it. 'The universe is broken and trying to find its way together again,' you said. I told you not only do I agree, when you put it that way, but it is no one person's responsibility to fix it."

"So there's no such thing as heroes?"

"No such thing."

I think of the things in the darkness between worlds. Can they somehow be watching? I remember their sounds.

"Your responsibility is to yourself," she says. "To live. To fix things about yourself if you see fit. No one person can carry the weight of the world. What did you want to ask me, dear?"

"Nothing. Nothing, Mom."

"Oh, and I don't care what your father says, I love your hair."

"Thanks, Mom. I love you too."

"How is that project of yours going?"

"Perfect, Mom. Just perfect."

I stare at the paper a while longer. The formulas and numbers are making sense to me. I add to the drawings. They are my drawings. I drew them. Or a ghost of me did. An American ghost in Zurich. Haunting Jaz. Haunting everyone. I understand now.

Pink? Pria chimes in via text. *Don't you think pink is so yesterday?*

Yeah, but it was something about yesterday I liked, I text back.

The board?

I don't care,

OK. I'll play, she texts. *This is the point in your story that is not a story, where you're supposed to go back in time to destroy the machine. Or decrypt a message from the past. No, the future. Maybe you right the wrongs in your life? Or make the world a better place? Resolve loose ends? Learn something? Teach someone?*

I let her text away. I text Jaz to come meet me. I sketch ideas and instructions on napkins while I wait.

"I see them too," I say, before he can say anything.

"You do?" he says. "What are you going to do?"

"I have some ideas."

"Like what?"

"Not sure."

"Not sure? Has it crossed your mind to destroy the machine, so it isn't used by that damn corporation?"

"I don't know. I think maybe I'm supposed to use it to send messages to myself."

"Anina."

"Or to you. Or for important things, like arranging to have hot chocolate served at Aeon's corporate meetings."

"Hmmm," he says. "Chocolate I can get behind. But aren't you afraid of tampering?"

"Nothing can be upset by tampering, because there is no tampering. There only is what is. No order. No divine law. No sin.

Only chaos."

"Why do you think that?" he asks.

I think of the presences in the void. There is no way to explain them to him. It crosses my mind that the unwritten songs by Seven Bells had to have crossed them to reach me during the disturbance on the plane. One of my ghosts was trying to reach me and brought a bit of a different future with her.

"Because you told me that, or something like it, once upon a time," I say. "When you told me why you quit your studies. Why you dropped out of everything."

"Oh. That's probably why it sounds good to me," he says. "I think it would make more sense with some absinthe."

"You were so bright, Jaz, you really were. I always loved that about you."

He looks like he is figuring an equation in his head.

"Anina, there were a lot of things I said to you that I regret."

We are both quiet.

"What happens now?" he asks.

"I think this is where you show me Zurich."

He takes me next door and buys a bottle of absinthe. The streets and shops of Zurich are better with him. His rooftop garden is better with his stories, stories of his life since we parted. I don't have many. Only the path that led me here. Foul tasting absinthe tastes better with him. I do not drink much. Soon I will be another story in his garden that will have one more bottle. When he has drunk himself to sleep I kiss his forehead and return to my hotel. I call Ilsa Hartlin to have someone pick me up.

Ilsa and I are alone in the cavern with the machine.

"I'm glad that you are back," she says. "You built a beautiful machine. We built a beautiful machine together."

"You were right," I say. "This is bigger than us."

She runs her hand along the smooth surface of the monolith.

"Oh what a sweet, sweet paradox it is," she says.

I pull the papers and napkins with my notes from my pockets.

"So what have you come up with?" she asks.

"I have my ideas."

"Your first one?"

"Fire it up. Let's find out just how much energy it takes to make a ghost that can interact."

She smiles.

5. Scatter

"What are you doing?" Jaz asks.

I didn't think he was awake yet. I close the door to his flat.

"Who was at the door?" he asks.

"Just giving myself instructions," I say.

"What?"

"You know, like you said. On how to destroy the machine."

67

"Anina," he says with a yawn. "Really?"

"What do you think?"

He lights a cigarette and prepares breakfast. Years of living like this has softened his sharp edges, but I'm not ready to trust him again. I'm not ready to leave him either.

He checks his stock portfolio on his tablet and brings two bowls of muesli and fruit to the table.

"What do you want to do today?" he asks.

I push two train tickets, courtesy of Aeon, across the table.

"Zurich is wonderful. How is the rest of Switzerland?"

"Beautiful."

At the train station I send Jaz for coffee. It is the time Ilsa and I arranged to rendezvous with one of my ghosts.

I see her by the ticket machine. She is young and looks at me like I am looking at her; searching her face for clues to something. Is she asking herself, *is this what becomes of me when I get old?* I was with Jaz at her age. I want to tell her so much but it takes so much energy to have her here. There is little time.

"Which one are you?" I ask.

"What do you mean?" the other me says.

"The machine. I'm supposed to—"

"Help me build it, of course," she says.

"Of course," I say.

I show her one of the napkins with my sketches and diagrams.

She looks at it, pockets it, and disappears into the crowd merging to go down the escalator leading to the trains.

"Who was that?" Jaz asks. He doesn't have coffee. He was watching. "Was that...you? It looked like you. What are you really doing?"

"Giving myself instructions on how to build the machine"

"But this morning, didn't you—"

"Give myself instructions on how to destroy it. Yes. And before that I gave myself instructions on how to sabotage it. And I'll give myself instructions on how to fix it later. I'll do all of it again a hundred times before I'm through."

He paces in a little circle.

"I see," he says. "Wow, you really aren't tampering at all. You're passing the buck."

"Your terminology is so unscientific. I love it."

"Is that what a scientist does? Is that what a—"

"Don't say hero. Say anything but hero, Jaz. Even scientist is better. Yes, I'm villainous. Say it. Vil-lain-ous."

He paces that little circle again. He has something to say. Is this the part in the story where he shows his awful side again?

"What?" I ask.

"Nothing," he says. "Except that I'm glad you're my villain."

I laugh.

"Why are you laughing?"

"Because I'm not yours," I say.

"No?"

"No. And also because you sounded like my dad just there."

"Ugh, no."

"Uh, yes."

"Do you think anyone else saw?" he asks.

"Probably. But no one but you knew what you were seeing."

No one but you can see me, I think. The music in the train station is distracting. It feels dissonant, though I know it is a simple melody. Since hearing the sound of the darkness, everything sounds different, but I know nothing has changed. The universe is still as fractured as it was at the moment of creation. Everything that ever was and ever will be is still shooting out in all directions from a single point. Will it keep expanding infinitely? Or, someday, will the pieces rubber-band back and reunite in a great destructive collapse. I try to recall those Seven Bells songs I heard on the plane, but all I can remember are the sounds of the darkness. I wish it didn't sound like laughter.

"What's going to happen?" Jaz asks.

"I don't know. Want to find out?"

He reaches for me. I close my hand around his.

DANIEL BRAUM

THE WATER DRAGON

I was still burning from the injustice at dinner last night when I got out of my car and felt the pressing afternoon heat. An ocean breeze, sullied with exhaust from rental cars and hotel shuttles buzzing along the two-lane road, found its way through the parking lot of the Aruban grocery store to my little patch of baking asphalt in the sun. Across the road, weathered palms towered over the dock-choked shore, silent watchers of the blue Caribbean water that hadn't yet forgotten how to sparkle.

Tranquility. Simplicity. Time in the sun with my husband. Mara and Jesse playing in the sand. Why did these things always seem so far away?

Seb meant well. The steakhouse had been recommended. The

wait staff was truly lovely and more important, kind and attentive to the kids. I almost didn't mind that a twenty-five percent service charge had been boldly added to our bill. Fair enough. But there was yet another blank line underneath it all for a tip.

I called over Hector, one of our waiters, and asked what the service charge was for.

"For the management," he said, the musical ring of his native Papiamento missing from his reply.

I could see traces of the beautiful local boy in the man before me. A smile like sunshine. Bronzed skin and bright eyes proclaiming that, like most Arubans, his heritage was from everywhere, a true child of the world.

"So that's not your tip?" I asked.

The uniformed staff innocuously went about their business of bussing tables and delivering food. I'd waited tables long ago, and knew they were listening or trying to. I could feel them straining to hear.

"No, ma'am," Hector said. "If you enjoyed your meal this evening and wish to tip us, that would be greatly appreciated."

"For the management, huh," I said. "That's not right. I can't imagine people wanting to tip twice."

His smile remained pleasant and professional but his eyes burned to say more. I sensed his silence was a practiced thing.

Management. The people who had been just part of the scenery on the way in stuck out now, dispelling my illusion of all-is-well-in-paradise.

A middle-aged lady in a floral sundress at the reservation stand watched the dining room with cold eyes. Three stocky men in suits, the only ones wearing jackets at all, sat at the bar chomping cigars, the curling smoke the same color as their slicked-back, thin hair. Their sense of separateness, a latent defect in my idyllic vision of island bliss, inspired the same disgust in my gut as if I'd just discovered rat droppings in the remnants of the sprinkled ice cream scoop Mara was sloshing around.

I knew from the news that Aruba was a place where a young American girl could disappear just like that. High-rise hotels were filled with those too rich and too insulated to give a shit about anything. It wasn't the only place justice could be bought, but these bloated restaurateurs were the actual faces of the proverbial "corrupt old sheriffs with the town under their sway." And we were eating at their table. Contributing to it all. And Sebastian didn't seem to mind.

"You're on vacation, Melanie, lighten up," he had said. "Just forget about it."

I had wanted to lecture him right then and there. I stared at Mara and Jesse finishing their ice cream, yearning for the Sebastian I thought I knew. Where was the bright-eyed lawyer who brilliantly used treaty rights to ensure an environmental impact study for San Diego's new sewage infrastructure? Where was the sexy man who could stand up against the water usage and river diversions of big agriculture in the afternoon and still make it to our date of watching the Perseids shoot through the August sky at Scripps

Cove?

Today I had wanted to wake him with soft kisses, whisper a singsong good morning, and run my hands all over his body, but when I opened my eyes I couldn't bear the sight of him. I told him I'm not going out to eat again and left him to supervise the kids' revelry on the twisty water slide by the pool outside our suite. Maybe roaming the aisles picking out the food we'd need for the next few days would cool me down.

The market was packed full of luxuries. Dutch chocolates. European cheeses. American brand-name cereals. The latest sports drinks. Iced display cases full of fresh fish. Everything a snowbird could need. I figured we'd make use of one of the pristine grills on the poolside lawn by our patio, so I started with burgers and chicken and snacks. After a few minutes I had filled the cart with about eighty bucks worth of stuff. Here I was in a grocery store when all I had wanted was a simple family vacation on the beach. Anywhere would have been fine. Anywhere simple. Just us and the kids. I would have even settled for something more upscale, like Cabo. But no, Seb wanted someplace different. Someplace fancy.

The checkout lines were painfully slow. A pair of middle-aged women with too much makeup and garish hair color jobs worked the only open registers. They slowly punched the old-fashioned cash registers with long, manicured nails and chitchatted in Dutch, pretending the tourists in line were invisible; generally giving the impression they owned the place, which they probably did.

A scrawny young girl packed my groceries. She looked Asian,

maybe Thai, and certainly didn't seem in place among the Dutch checkout ladies. I didn't like the way she didn't meet their eyes. She struck me as a scavenger, a small reef fish that survived by cleaning fins and teeth, tolerated by the bigger, predatory fish for her usefulness. I didn't doubt for a second these women would sweep the girl aside, uncaring as the sea, or gobble her up if the situation warranted. I took out four twenties to pay and get the hell out.

"Forty dollars and twenty-six cents," the checkout lady said.

I'd mistakenly thought the prices were marked in U.S. dollars so the total was half what I'd expected. As I pocketed my two twenties I realized someone was speaking.

"May I please bring your groceries to the car?"

It was the young girl. Politely standing there waiting for an answer.

"No, thank you. I can manage," I said.

My thoughts drifted to a little puffer fish I had found as a child in one of the tide pools on the beach after a summer storm. Its bright yellows and white-and-brown leopard-like spots marked it as a denizen of tropical waters far away; out of place among the silver-gray Atlantic dwellers my friends and I were used to. I put it in a cup, took it home, and gave it to Mrs. Wells, the grandmotherly old woman who kept a salt-water tank much to the delight of all the kids on the block. She was warm in a way I doubted these women were capable of.

"Please, ma'am. I just want to let you know we work for tips only," the scrawny girl said, turning her face away so the checkout lady wouldn't hear.

I knew nothing I could do could save this girl, but I wanted to make this moment, this day's work a bit easier for her.

"Okay, come on," I said.

I took the heavier bag and allowed the girl to take the other. We crossed the lot. I opened the rental minivan's doors and placed the bags inside. The girl stood there with that practiced, polite waiting stance.

I took the two twenties out of my pocket and gave them to her. I just wanted to. Part of me expected to see some sort of visible shift, a clue, a confirmation that I had been played, but the girl just held the bills and looked confused.

"Put it away," I said before she could speak.

She slowly folded the money, as if giving me time to change my mind, and put the bills in her pocket. Her grateful please-take-me-home eyes were why I avoided animal shelters, but something more lurked in their murky-brown depths.

"Wait," she said.

I figured *now* would come the plea for more money. I had no problem saying no, but I felt if she asked me to take her home, to take her away from this, I might actually just do so. She sprinted to the dumpster by the side of the store and returned with a small plastic bucket sloshing with water.

"Take this, please," she said.

I wondered what it could be. A gift? A pet? Some island

delicacy?

"It doesn't belong here," she said.

Just like you don't, I thought and peered inside. Chunks of white coral surrounded what I took to be a brightly painted Easter egg.

"I found it on the beach," she said. "I can't take care of it."

This wasn't the cry for help I'd been expecting. I worried that my generosity had pegged me for an easy mark and she had rushed to grab something, anything, to sell me. But she was so solemn and sincere and not asking for anything. If this was a put-on, she deserved an Academy Award.

She took the fist-sized, oval thing out of the water and handed it to me. I held it up to the sun. Mica pinks and iridescent greens and silvers glistened in the light. The blues were so bright I thought that my first impression was right and it really was some sort of a fake egg. Then something shifted inside and it undulated like a sea anemone in a gentle current.

"It's going to hatch soon," she said. "It needs a mommy."

It pulsed again, and for an instant my hand was covered in its shifting opal pinks and blues and greens. My mind filled with images of fledgling geese following their mothers. Schools of silver fish turning in unison. Baby sandpipers following older ones on the shore.

The girl looked pleased. She turned around and walked across the lot, stopping outside the automatic doors to ask if she could carry someone's bags.

I wanted to call her back and ask what this thing was, but the heat was really getting to me and I yearned for a drink.

"Your bucket," was all I managed to say. It was empty and dry. The egg felt smooth and right in my hand.

"Don't need it anymore," she answered, and then stepped inside, the sliding doors closing behind her with a whoosh.

I took the pail and "egg" back to the hotel and put it in the corner of our patio next to a lush green bush, its tropical pink blooms alive with lazy butterflies.

Empty lounge chairs surrounded the courtyard swimming pool. Each had been shifted to face the sun, a daily tropism enacted by occupants now gone except for one old couple soaking in the last rays before the sunset. Juvenile iguanas, their bright, baby-green skin already fading to mottled gray, crossed the lawn, tails dragging, returning to their homes in the landscaping. Jesse ran from Seb's side at the barbeque to chase one foraging for scraps of lettuce and tomato from our table.

Our neighbors from two suites down were departing for dinner with cleaned and fully dressed children in tow. Mara, still in her bathing suit, looked up from her coloring book and watched them go with a long face. I brought Seb buns to toast on the grill.

"You're going to explain to them why we're not going out tonight," he said.

"It was your idea to go to Aruba," I said.

"Please. Can't you just let it go? We're on vacation."

"Would you stand for this back in L.A.? No."

"But we're not in L.A."

"What's the difference?" I asked.

"We're on vacation."

"Come on, Seb," I said.

I wanted to remind him of the Vietnamese restaurant where his entire office wouldn't eat because of pay disputes with workers, but behind him, on the patio, a flash of color caught my eye. The plastic pail was turned over.

A ribbon of color fluttered in the bush. I couldn't take my eyes off it. I walked over to investigate. Seb, probably thinking I had let it go, went back to burger-flipping duty. An eel-like creature as thick as my arm was wriggling in the branches. I could kind of see through it. Its bright blues were much too fluorescent to be real, yet there it was pulsing like the egg in the parking lot, gaining substance and getting larger with each undulation. I thought of butterfly wings filling with blood; gaining shape and color. Four small appendages, more like fins than limbs, jutted from its body, two at its side, and two at the base of its tail. Tight rows of scales sparkled with hints of pink and oranges where the sun hit it. It writhed and turned, and I found myself nose to nose with a cat-like face augmented with horns and whiskers and budding knobby protuberances, a New Year dragon in miniature straight out of some Chinatown parade. It hovered there, buzzing with contentment, regarding me with eyes like mica, shifting layers of color—seaside hues, the blues and silvers and glistening pinks of the ocean.

"Mama, Mama?" Jesse called.

"What's wrong? Don't you hear him calling you?" Seb asked.

The dragon hissed at the sound of his voice.

I shooed it as if it were a neighborhood dog that had gotten too close to my kids. With a blur like a kite twisting in the wind, it disappeared.

"What are you doing, Mama?" Jesse asked.

"Nothing, sweetheart," I said.

Remnants of the cracked egg lay on the ground, a ring of dried up brown leaves and parched soil around it.

I sat the kids down at the table and Seb served the burgers.

The dragon rose behind him, its blues and greens glowing in the late-day sun like a giant hummingbird, hovering there silently. I took a step to the side. It shifted position. I thought of the sand pipers on the beach and took another step. It matched my movements. Again.

"You okay?" Seb asked.

I nodded, nibbling on a burger, watching the dragon float there, staring at me, its fish-like eyes never blinking. I hoped it would just go away.

The ground sprinklers turned on, spraying a mist of water on the lawn and bushes near us. The dragon didn't move. A passing maintenance man cursed into his radio and started tinkering with the sprinkler farthest away from us.

Seb moved his chair to avoid getting wet.

"Tomorrow we go out to dinner," Seb said, under his breath. "This is no way to show the kids a good time."

A terrible hiss filled the air; a sound perfectly matching how pissed off I was at Seb. I thought it was the water pressure turned up, but the maintenance man was standing up triumphantly. The sprinklers had halted; plump water droplets were drying up on the trees and leaves, like in a fast-motion film.

The dragon's mouth was slightly open, the source of the awful sound, I realized. Back home at work one of the board members of River Watch had a pet boa constrictor. It tamely and docilely rode around his neck, even at our sustainable development meetings with county agencies. One day something pissed it off out of the blue and it hissed like a burst steam vent. I didn't think such a loud sound could come from a four-foot creature. This was much worse.

I stood up, thinking I should shoo it away, back it off, only I leaned closer to Seb testing to see if it would follow, all the while knowing that it would. And it did.

A nimble little iguana crawled up the table and seized the opportunity to steal a mouthful of juicy tomato from Mara's plate.

Jesse squealed with joy, and Mara screamed like a princess.

"Shoo," I said. "Damn lizard. Get away."

A blur of color whirled onto the plate. The lizard flew into the air and landed on the dry lawn with a pathetic croak.

Both kids were screaming now. Seb scrambled out of his chair, on guard.

He checked that the kids were okay, then examined the lizard.

"It's dead," he said, holding the dried-up, withered thing by the tail.

I looked at the dragon, the weight of my anger and frustration upon it. It simply disappeared.

"What happened?" Seb asked, more to himself than to me. "Poor thing's completely crisped. Dehydrated."

"I want to go to Benihana," Mara said through a sob.

"We'll go, tomorrow," Seb said.

The dragon appeared behind him, a ribbon of color unfurling with the breeze. It hovered there. Like a dog testing its leash. Testing my resolve.

We brought the kids inside, calmed them down and distracted them with DVDs and playtime in the tub before bed. I thought of the little girl at the store. Before long Mara would be her age. Was she working right now?

I could feel the dragon. Outside in the dark. Wanting to come in. Seething like I was. I thought I should go outside and chase it away. Instead I lay down on the bed. Seb joined me. We fell asleep without words. Without touching. Above the covers and with the lights on.

I woke, listening for the sound of birds, my eyes not fully open. Daylight crept in through the blinds giving the room a warm glow. In my peripheral vision I saw Seb next to me, on his back and snoring softly. Something luminous and blue floated over him. The dragon, I realized. It shone with its own light and had grown almost as long as the bed. Silent and dreamlike and out of place in the morning sun and crisp bedroom whites. I watched, the world still soft and fuzzy. Every few seconds its body undulated, a kite gently rippling in unseen wind.

My cat sometimes brought me mice from the yard, waiting for approval for the kill. I knew, as surely as I knew when Jesse was sick or Mara was in danger, that this thing wanted that same kind of approval. Approval to make Seb dead. Dead like the lizard last night. Dried out and sucked free of life.

My mind raced back to when our marriage was a new and fragile thing. While home shopping, Seb and I had fought over which house to choose and where to raise our family. He told me then that it is the choices we make in our darker moments that define us. It is how we act during our struggles, when things are not easy, that really count.

The dragon hovered. Glided around Seb. Hovered some more. With just a word. A thought. All my anger. All my rage would be released. The dragon would do that for me. And I knew it would feel so good.

Sweat beaded on Seb's forehead as he slept. His skin looked pale, his dark hair less substantial. I felt he was just a shape of a man. Unconscious and fading slowly. I thought of how happy he had been the first time he saw our future home. His eyes jubilant and full of spark. Nothing could break his joy. Not my grim outbursts. Not the superstitious lectures of our broker, Mrs. Kim.

Consequences come with acquisition, she had said. Power and energy is exchanged in all transactions big and small. Why have you not investigated your house history and the fortunes of the sellers?

I'm looking forward, not back, Seb had joyfully told her. This is the place we will raise our family. I dismissed Mrs. Kim's feng shui notions and filed them away in the clutter of my mind, a forgotten seed come to life by the heat of this moment. Now I heard her in my mind admonishing me about helping the little girl. Should I have just let her be? Let her fend for herself on the reef? Given back her gift or not accepted it at all? I never dumped my change into the charity cans at the market or helped street urchins that tugged on my heartstrings. I knew giving to professional efforts was the way to go. So why this?

No good deed goes unpunished, I often told Seb. Especially when he would take on too much pro bono work. Good deeds open doors, was his counter. Sometimes they aren't easy or don't seem to be what we want, but they are the first steps on courses of action that are just and right.

The dragon rippled and cooed contently, as if I were telling a bedtime story. Seb snored away beneath it. Had he drifted so far from his ideals? Grown soft. Fat. Blind. Had his boundaries become walls?

I thought of the puffer I had given to old Mrs. Wells. It was a crazy thing, but that little fish thrived in its new, artificial home. It grew large and healthy along with the little blue ones that were just supposed to live a short while to kick-start the biology of the tank. It was there whenever I visited and as far as I knew was still alive today. It defied everything I knew about foreign species. Most were invasive and caused awful messes. Like the snakes introduced to the Hawaiian Islands by cargo ship that decimated the defenseless birds that had evolved without them. Or the cane toads and flies plaguing Australia. Or European fish messing up the ecosystem of Midwestern lakes and rivers. Rivers were the last things I wanted to think about right now. I had wanted the water rights struggles of work to be left behind this vacation. I had hoped to trade the tangle of aqueducts and legal wrangling and power brokering that allowed the water to flow for the sound of gentle waves. The frustrating reality that cities like Los Angeles and Las Vegas by nature should not exist were haunting me even here.

On the floor, three of the house geckos that patrolled our walls for bugs lay dead like last night's iguana. I sprung out of bed, my instincts demanding I check on the kids. I dashed into their room. The dragon followed. Thankfully they were still sleeping soundly. The dragon floated from Mara to Jesse, its body rippling faster in a way I perceived as inquisitive.

"No," I said. "Get away. Shoo."

It's what I should have said finding it above Seb. But it didn't budge. It just floated there. Rippling. Testing me to see if I really meant it.

"I said go."

"Who are you talking to?" Seb called from the other room.

I swatted at the dragon. I yelled, shooing it into the hall just as

Seb emerged from the bedroom.

"What's going on?" he asked. "Are you all right?"

With one final overhead swipe I chased the dragon out the sliding doors, into the morning light.

"Nothing," I said.

"Don't tell me nothing," he said. "What the hell are you doing?"

I hadn't smoked since my college days when I was dating Seb, but I wanted a cigarette right now. Along with a stiff tropical drink. Outside the lawn looked brownish and dry. The sunlight was not sparkling on the pool like most mornings. I thought of Sebastian that sunny afternoon driving from San Diego to Los Angeles when it dawned on me that he was the one for me. United in our love and our passion, we thought we would make a better future, our vision flowing from us, from our bond, out into the world. I felt myself welling up with tears.

"Seb. I don't know. It's just this weird thing happened at the store yesterday."

"What?" he asked.

And I heard all I needed to. His tone was the one he reserved for my "histrionics." I hated the disdain. I wasn't going to justify this to him. Not now. But I wanted to yell. I wanted to get in his face and scream, "Look at you. Look at who you've become."

But I said, "Never mind. It's nothing."

He paced back and forth in front of the door. Was the water level in the pool lower?

"Listen. I'm sorry," Seb said. "If you want to eat in the room, then okay. And about the other night. You're right. I'm always fighting other people's battles so I guess the part of me that really wanted a holiday turned my brain off. I'll shop. I'll go to the store so you don't have to."

I looked past him, out the door. It was easier to see through him now. On the lawn were more dead iguanas. The big bush looked wilted. Its flowers devoid of butterflies. The dragon rose out of the swimming pool. An old couple and a maintenance man peered into the deep end, looking perplexed. The dragon's horns were more pronounced. Razor-sharp. Its whiskers ended in rapier point tips.

"No, Seb. I'll go," I said. "There's something I have to do."

The young girl wasn't working and the checkout ladies weren't any help. They told me no such girl worked there, no doubt fearing I was some sort of immigration authority or just an American causing trouble.

I unleashed a flurry of profanities and stormed up and down the aisles. Seething mad. The dragon followed. Floating above the aisles. Its head just a few feet over my shoulder and now fifteen feet of shark-thick torso trailing behind. Bottles of soda bubbled as we passed.

I stopped in front of a stock boy neatly stacking bottles of lemon Perrier. He didn't react to the dragon. No one in the store did. I didn't care.

"Excuse me. I'm looking for a young girl. About this high. Not from here," I said.

He said nothing, just looked over my shoulder with concern. A manager, a Dutch man in a short-sleeved dress shirt, was heading our way.

"May I help you?" the manager asked.

"I'm looking for a girl. A young scrawny thing. Plastic pail."

"Yes, ma'am. The ladies told me. There is no such girl here. Maybe you have us mistaken for the Tropic Mart?"

"No, I have not," I said, loud enough to cause a young couple, their cart full of wine and cheese and fruit, to veer away.

"Ma'am, please. Can we talk in my office, or outside if you prefer?"

"Certainly. As soon as you tell me where that little girl is," I yelled.

The dragon circled above him. It was big enough to swallow him whole. I could feel it wanting to. I wanted it to. And I wasn't sure I could control it if I tried.

"Ma'am, I'm going to have to ask you to leave."

The dragon thrashed. Soda bottles fell to the floor. Through the big windows I saw a police car in the lot. The checkout ladies were talking to an officer and pointing my way.

I called Seb on my cell. Mineral water bubbled and foamed among green broken glass. The officer clomped up the aisle.

The dragon dove to the floor. It slithered on the slick linoleum and reared its face to mine, like yesterday in the bush. Its whiskers arced toward me, the sharp tips reaching as if guided by an irresistible current. I thought it might bite me or stab me with its whisker tips, but it just brushed my face, the gentle caress of a deadly anemone to a clownfish.

With each pinprick touch, I knew I was wrong. Wrong for trying to bring it back.

Sebastian answered the phone. "Mel? Is everything all right?"

"I'm okay, hold on a second, dear."

The dragon circled. A shark. A bird of prey. A cat. But it was no earthly animal. It was a dragon. My dragon. I shared its disdain for the police, for this store, for this island and its earthbound ways.

"What's going on here?" the officer asked.

I could sic it on them. It would eat them whole. Suck them dry.

"I think there is some sort of mistake," I said calmly and demurely. "I was just shopping."

The dragon had found *me*. Touched *me*. I knew it wouldn't let me leave with this officer. It hovered above us, rippling gently, its colors even brighter in the fluorescence.

The manager and officer looked at each other, asking each other in some secret, inaudible local language if I was worth the trouble.

I turned and walked away. They weren't worth *my* trouble. But I knew what was.

"Sorry, Seb, I was just leaving the store," I said, into the phone.

"What was all that?" Seb asked. "Are you okay?"

His voice transmitted crystal clear but he felt a million miles away. A voice speaking somewhere in the darkness of a vast tunnel.

"Everything's fine, honey," I said. "But listen. I've decided I want to go out to dinner. To the steakhouse from the other day."

The couple across the table from us, Ernie and Constance Reegan, were from Orange County and occupied the suite two rooms down from ours. Ernie owned a few car dealerships and was as wide as a Winnebago. He blathered on about his high rolling at the casinos. Connie was tall and pretty, or at least was beneath her makeup and Botox. She said she sat on the boards of a few charities I hadn't heard of. She wasn't shy about sharing her extensive knowledge of Aruba's shopping spots and many spas. Their kids numbly sipped Shirley Temples and made messes with mozzarella sticks along with Mara and Jesse while we adults waited for our steaks.

The dragon barely fit in the room. Its silvery underside brushed the tops of the waitstaff's heads. One dive and belly roll, one thrashing fit, was all it would take.

"So I put the rest of my stack on twenty-eight," Ernie said. "I figured my luck couldn't be bad all night and it's Connie and I's number. What comes out? Twenty-seven."

"Seb and I don't play much."

"Oh, you should," he said, taking out a cigar. "It's not Vegas, but it'll do."

"Nothing's like Vegas," Connie said. "You should see the lobby of the Marriott though. They just remodeled it."

A stocky Aruban man, "management," came over from the bar and lit Ernie's cigar.

"Enjoy your meal, Mr. Reegan," the man said.

"We come here a lot," Connie whispered to me.

Seb fidgeted in his chair and even the kids looked uncomfortable with the long silence. I looked around for Hector, our bright-eyed waiter from last time.

"So," Connie said valiantly trying to make conversation. "Did you hear on the news about that girl who disappeared? Natalee Holloway. They're going to try and get the case going again."

"She's only getting this attention because she's a pretty American with rich parents," Seb said. "There's no justice."

"You can't buy it," Connie said.

"If it was my kid, I'd tear up the island," Ernie said, cigar in his mouth. "Nothing I wouldn't do for my kids. Nothing. They mean the world to me. The rest of the world can go to hell."

I looked at the dragon. Was Natalee Holloway at the bottom of the ocean? Had the same currents that brought it here swept her body out to sea? Did the management care, beyond the notion that a dead American and a botched investigation was bad for tourism? Ernie and Connie and even Seb didn't care enough to change their vacation plans. Maybe Ernie was a good man. Maybe the management were kind souls, and maybe everyone here was like Seb, just doing their jobs and wanting some time in the sun.

Maybe their jobs were even noble ones. They provided for their own and protected their own and the rest of the world could go to hell like Ernie said. Fair enough. Seemed enough. But it wasn't. It's why the dragon came to me.

"Please excuse me," I said.

"You okay?" Seb asked.

"Just need some air. Don't mind me."

I went outside and turned the corner into the alley by the kitchen door and lit up a cigarette.

The dragon spiraled in the air above the rooftops of the neighboring buildings. With a word I could send it down. Crushing the restaurant.

I closed my eyes, savoring the thought along with a deep pull from the cigarette. When I opened my eyes, Hector, our waiter from the other night, was next to me leaning up against the wall, smoking. The kitchen door was still closed.

"Beautiful," he said, watching the circling dragon.

"Yes," I said.

"I think it is parched," he said. "Drinking only sweat and booze and our bland desalinated water."

"It doesn't belong here. Does it?" I said.

"Nope."

"Where's it from?"

"Doesn't matter. Someplace with lots of fresh water, I guess," he said. "There are no rivers here. What about where you live?"

"We have aqueducts bringing water from the mountains to the

desert. From north to south. From state to state. Some of them are dammed. And diverted."

"Dragon would like it there," he said.

"I imagine it would," I said.

"It's getting big. It might not listen to you anymore, especially after you let it loose for a while. You might only get one shot."

He was right. I wasn't sure how much longer I could control the dragon.

"So you gonna do this?" he asked.

"Yes," I said.

I took another big pull from my cigarette and when I turned to look, Hector was gone. Just me and the silent dragon and the sounds of the kitchen pots banging and oil frying and meat grilling from the kitchen. The door still closed. The alley empty.

I pictured the restaurant in flames. It would feel so good to see the dragon rising from the smoke, glistening from the dousing water. But I had a better idea. The dragon finding me was something special. There had to be a reason. I wanted to make it count.

I went inside and told Seb not to worry but I had to leave and that he should stay and finish the dinner with the kids. I took a taxi back to the hotel and packed my bags for our flight in the morning. I sat on the porch and smoked another cigarette. The dragon was almost all grown-up. I didn't think it needed me anymore but still I sensed it didn't want me to go. But I had to. And I had one thing to ask of it.

Our plane raced through the clouds; a marvel of aeronautics and physics and human will shuttling our vacation-tanned butts through the sky. The dragon sailed alongside, its blues more electric than the endless sky, arms tucked in, whiskers plastered to its face, tail straight back.

Work continued as if I had never left. Northern California was saber-rattling about a ballot initiative to break away from the south. Every user along the Colorado River had a grievance about their share of the flow. Our cities were sucking the water, sucking the energy from our neighbors. Our community was an abomination. Part of the problem. And there was no real solution. Until now.

I drove Mara and Jesse to and from school, and to and from their after-school happenings along our streets, lush with green lawns and flowering trees. The desert that now was Los Angeles never looked so abundant. Seb was working a case. Some good cause or another. We were back from the island and at the end of the day we all came home. To our house. Our castle. Our palace hooked up to the grid, sucking juice in splendorous isolation like everyone else on the block. Everyone else in the development. Like everyone else.

The dragon hovered over our property. It was so big. And even more out of place here than in Aruba. Maybe here it would be happy. Maybe here it would have purpose.

"We could have stayed there, I know," I told it. "You would

have sucked that island dry. But what would that have accomplished?"

Surely it could see or smell the ocean. Or sense its way back home to wherever it came. But it was meant for me. Meant for this.

Mara and Jesse were sleeping soundly. Seb was gently snoring. I thought of waking them to say goodbye, but they felt so far away. So transparent. Part of the quiet darkness all around them. I took the keys and drove into the night. The dragon followed. Soon the suburbs gave way to long stretches of highway, and then to lonely desert roads the sprawl hadn't yet crept over.

A stretch of aqueduct towered over the scrub and asphalt, molded concrete veins feeding the city the thousands of gallons of water rushing past us every second.

"Go on," I said to the dragon.

It hesitated. Stars sparkled above. In the distance I thought I could see the city lights, shimmering unaware.

"I know you thirst. And I don't think there's enough water for you and the city. There can't be. But that's okay. Drink."

It hovered above the rushing water, scales shifting to the color of desert night.

"Drink," I said.

It submerged itself. I held my breath.

A MAN'S GUIDE TO COSTUMES AND THE MOST COMMON WAYS TO GET ARRESTED

(written with Jason Sileo)

1. Hotel Room Parties in Las Vegas

The roomful of grown-ups in costumes were carrying on like children. Just like Ed had expected the day after Halloween to be like. His brother was the worst offender.

"I know why you're here," a woman Ed didn't know said to him. "You're here to take off your costume."

He didn't know *anyone* in this godforsaken room party. Except for his brother Oscar. That was the point. To break out of the post-prison blues, Oscar had said.

"I'm not wearing a costume," Ed said.

He wore what he always wore since getting out. Black faded jeans. Motorcycle boots. Different shirt though. Thin cotton and short sleeves for the Las Vegas heat.

The woman looked at him as if she didn't believe him and as if he was indeed wearing some outlandish rubber mask and costume. Her face was painted to look like a sugar skull. Her black shirt with bones on it exposed the bottom of her concave belly and skin the color of coffee with milk. A tattoo of a scythe marked her upper thigh. Skirt much too short. Ink much too sharp. Much too bright. Either new. Or fake.

"Like my costume?" Oscar tapped the silver milk bowl he wore around his neck on a chain. "I'm milk! Here, kitty kitty."

He looked ridiculous in his white T-shirt and white sweatpants, but he was right, there were at least four women dressed as black cats. All of them looking fine. The woman standing next to Miss Sugar Skull looking particularly fine all in tight, black clothes hugging her slender body. She smiled at Oscar as she swayed and mouthed song lyrics of the bass-heavy tune cranking from the little speaker on the desk with the hard liquor. The out-of-date hotel suite was packed with guests holding red plastic cups. Over-tipping the Flamingo's monkey-suited bellhop made Oscar feel like a big man. Ed didn't blame him for wanting to take him to a party now that he was out. Ed recognized the bellhop's jailhouse ink and knew he would have told them where the parties were anyway. The two men had seen something in each other; was it the telltale costume of an ex-con, the cloud that follows those who have known hardship? Or just a recognition they were different than all the soft people surrounding them?

"Why are *you* here?" Ed asked Miss Sugar Skull.

"I'm here for you, Eduardo," she said.

He hadn't heard a woman speak his name since...since Francisca. Before he could ask the woman what she meant, her cat-suited friend screeched and grabbed Oscar.

"*Oooh. Leche con azúcar. Baila conmigo!*" Cat-Suited Woman said.

"What?" Oscar said with a big goofy smile. "What's she saying? What's she saying, Ed?"

"Dance with me! Dance with me," Cat-Suited Woman said. "I'm *here* with her but I'm *not* here for your brother."

When she smiled one cheek rose higher than the other and she wore too much makeup. Her eyes sparkled against the fluorescent pink glare coming through the window from the casino across the street. Ed knew she was the kind of girl that was dangerous. Dangerous for Oscar. She'd break his heart. And Oscar might be stupid enough to let her.

"Let's do this. You here to dance?" Oscar asked.

"I'm here to party," Cat-Suited Woman said.

"My brother Ed's here to party. Ed come on. Be friendly. Dance with us."

"I don't dance," Ed said.

"Don't worry. He's not a psycho ex-con despite his clever

disguise," Oscar said. "He's a teddy bear."

Cat-Suited Woman took Oscar by the hand and led him into the crowd of sexy nurses, cat suits, zombies, and male stripper wannabes.

Miss Sugar Skull reached for Ed's hand.

"I mean it. I don't dance," Ed said. "I'm just the milk's older brother."

The woman leaned in and whispered, "I know who you are."

Her black T-shirt, with the skeleton on it, clung to her body. Raised glitter outlined the bones. White makeup covered her face. Little, red roses surrounded her blackened eyes. A simple spider web adorned her forehead and neat stitches extended her mouth to her cheeks.

Her breath felt cool on his face. A hint of something earthy and sweet lingered beneath the burnt chemical scent of her face makeup.

"You really know who I am?" Ed asked. "So, tell. Who am I?"

Across the room Oscar and Cat-Suited Woman danced in the costumed crowd. His hands traced the jaguar-spot tattoos on her shoulder. The room smelled like decades of smoke. And alcohol-laced sweat.

"You're a man who doesn't want to be here," Miss Sugar Skull said. "Your brother convinced you to come. To party. So you did. But you're here for something else. Your brother promised you'd be back in time to check in with your P.O. in the morning. So you listened."

Ed's instincts screamed danger but he knew she wasn't a cop. Cops didn't smell like a church during a funeral.

"So what is it I'm here for?" Ed asked.

"I'll show you. I'm getting my sister and your brother and I'll show you."

Before Ed could question her a blonde woman with black-framed glasses dressed as a cop pushed through the door. She confidently walked on too-tall spiked heels and wore a square hat. Silver handcuffs hung off the belt circling her black leather pants. Ed noticed the ring on her finger sparkling, even in the dim light. And the hint of white powder under her nose.

"Hey there. If I don't get a beer soon I'm gonna have to arrest someone," the sexy cop said.

"In the bathroom," Ed said.

The sexy cop stepped closer. Too close. He could feel the heat of her body.

"Help a lady out?" she said. "How about you get me one. And I think about not giving you a ticket."

Ed moved away from her and hurried into the bathroom. She had been close enough to touch. The smell of her. Her breath. Her warmth. All intoxicating. For a heartbeat he had forgotten Francisca. Vegas was proving dangerous. Parties. One of the most common ways to get arrested. Trouble. Capital T. Ed reached into the bathtub to grab a bottle, grateful for the chill from the icy water. The door shut behind him. The sexy cop leaned against it unbuttoning her shirt.

"Nice ring," Ed said. "Open the door. I don't want any trouble."

"It's Halloween. In Vegas."

She unbuttoned the last button revealing a pink bra with a small bag of cocaine tucked inside one cup.

"Halloween was yesterday. But points for partying hard. Just open the door. I don't mess around with other people's old ladies."

Her confused expression changed to resignation.

"Fine, but you're not leaving without doing a line with me."

The door burst open. A short, stocky guy with muscles stretching his khaki shorts and polo shirt barreled in looking like he was having a heart attack.

"What the fuck, Kerrie?" he said.

"Easy, man," Ed said. "I'm just grabbing a beer."

"Get the *fuck* away from my wife."

He rushed past his bra-clad wife and pushed Ed. Ed staggered and fell onto the toilet. He tried to stand but the guy was on him. Strong hands closed around Ed's neck and squeezed. Ed punched the guy's back. He planted his feet and tried to push up. Everything was blurring and getting dark. He reached for something. Anything. His left hand plunged into the ice-filled bathtub. His fingers closed round a bottle and he swung it up.

The crash was unreal. Like a sound effect but the hiss and smell of hops and foam was as real as could be. The guy staggered back with his hands over his face. Blood poured from between his fingers. Onlookers from the party pulled the wailing man out of the bathroom. A jagged shard of the broken bottle stuck out of his right cheek.

Miss Sugar Skull rushed into the bathroom. Oscar and Cat-Suited Woman right behind her.

"Do something," Cat-Suited Woman said.

"No," Miss Sugar Skull said.

"Everyone sees. It's gonna ruin the party."

"What?" Oscar said. "What's she going to do? You okay?"

"We're not here to party," Miss Sugar Skull said. "Let's go."

Ed rubbed his neck. Cell phones were out. Dialing. And snapping photos.

"She's right," Ed said. "We gotta get out of here."

She was right. No way he was going back in over Oscar's plan to break him out of the same old, same old. It took everything he had to keep his head down and nose clean in there.

He followed his brother and the girls out of the party and down the long winding hall to the elevator. After what seemed like an eternal wait the car came and they entered. Miss Sugar Skull pushed the G button.

"This is bad, Ed. Your P.O.'s gonna flip," Oscar said.

"It's gonna be all right," Cat-Suited Woman said. "Don't kill the buzz. We're just moving the party."

The elevator stopped at the ground level and they exited to the concrete parking garage beneath the casino.

Ed sat behind the wheel.

"No," Miss Sugar Skull said. "You're too drunk."

"Right," Ed said.

He switched seats with Oscar.

"Where to?" Oscar asked.

"Just get out of here," Ed said. "Then home."

Oscar put the car in reverse, spun the wheels, and cruised out the exit taking them away from the casino and the shitstorm up in the suite.

2. Traffic Stops

Oscar swung it onto Las Vegas Boulevard.

"Where to?" he asked.

"Home," Ed said. "Take it west. I need to be home."

"No. East," Miss Sugar Skull said.

Oscar gripped the wheel and spun the car around.

"Why the fuck'd you do that?" Ed said.

"Don't know," Oscar said.

"Turn it back."

"I can't."

"Aw, you're going to ruin the party aren't you?" Cat-Suited Woman said to her sister.

"His ex-wife said to head east," Miss Sugar Skull said.

"I ain't ruining my party for this guy's ex-wife."

"Are they talking about my wife?" Ed asked Oscar.

He pictured her still and lifeless. Lying on the rest stop concrete. Her dark hair a bloody tangle surrounding her bruised face.

"I dunno," Oscar said. "I'll get you home."

"Yeah? We need to go west. I have to get back to L.A. before my P.O. realizes I left the state."

"Everyone just relax," Miss Sugar Skull said. "You *can't* go home yet."

"At least slow down," Ed said. "Speeding's one of the most common ways for a guy like me to get arrested."

Red and blue lights flashed in the rearview mirror.

"Fuck. Speak of the devil," Ed said.

Oscar pulled the car onto the right shoulder and put it in park.

"Be cool," Ed said.

The cruiser pulled behind them. A cop exited and strutted over.

"You know why I pulled you over?"

"Speeding?" Oscar answered.

"Affirmative, amigo."

Ed hated the cop's condescending tone.

"License and registration."

Oscar retrieved the documents from the glove box and handed them over.

"Do something," Cat-Suited Woman said to her sister. "This is ruining the party."

"Officer," Miss Sugar Skull said. "Wait."

The cop turned to her and put his hand on his holster. When they made eye contact he froze. Something passed between them. Ed thought of the black-and-white swirl at the beginning of *Twilight Zone* episodes he and Francisca loved to watch on New

Year's Day. But there was nothing. Just the woman's soft amber pupils reflecting the light of the waning moon.

The cop returned the documents.

"Look, you better slow down," he stammered. "Be careful when you pull out. You all have a good evening." He entered his cruiser and drove off.

Oscar merged back into traffic. "What the fuck was that?"

"You won't understand," Miss Sugar Skull said. "Just thank us you didn't get busted."

"I-I can't even," Ed said. "You gotta tell me what the fuck that just was."

"Doesn't matter. Some things just don't matter. Okay?"

"No. Not okay. But pull over. I gotta take a piss. That sure as hell matters."

"Wait till we hit the open road," Miss Sugar Skull said.

Ed didn't have to go. He was thinking of making a run for it. Something was going on here. Something that spelled trouble.

Las Vegas's lights gave way to the starkness of the desert highway. Miss Sugar Skull nodded her permission and Oscar pulled over. Ed opened the door and slammed it behind him.

Cacti taller than Ed lined both sides of the road. The day's heat still radiated off the ground. He walked between the cacti careful not to snag himself, stopped in a clearing, and unzipped his pants.

A tiny pair of eyes stared at him from the cactus arm before him. A black lizard with an orange-and-yellow pattern on its back basked on the cactus watching him. Ed turned away and relieved himself.

A sting jabbed the back of his arm. He turned to see the lizard scuttling away on the sand. It stopped, turned its head, flicked its tongue at him, and then continued fleeing.

He checked his arm. There were two neat red dots.

"Fuck me," Ed said. He zipped his pants and made his way back to the car.

He opened the passenger door and buckled his seatbelt.

"You're not going to let us go west are you?" Ed asked.

"No," Miss Sugar Skull said. "But there's a motel a few miles up. We can stop there."

"Yesssssss. Party," Cat-Suited Woman said. "My milk still warm?"

Oscar scrunched his face and shrugged. Then he said, "Hell yeah."

Ed's arm hurt bad but he made no mention of the bite or the dizziness he was feeling.

Fucking lizard, he thought. I've shaken off worse than this.

On the side of the road he saw people walking among the tall cacti but said nothing about them either.

3. Motel Rooms in Las Vegas

Oscar drove the Charger too fast through the motel parking lot.

A neon vacancy sign flashed in front of the old, low-rise

building. A procession of about a dozen ghost- and skeleton-costumed people danced among the parked cars under the two a.m. sky. Ed struggled to make out the colors of their costumes but they all seemed gray.

"Careful. You're going to hit them," Ed said.

"Who?" Oscar asked.

The costumed dancers were gone.

Oscar stopped the car by the little office and they piled out. An old man drank from a bottle labeled Rattle-Shake Chocolate Milk.

"Two rooms, please," Cat-Suited Woman said.

"Two?" Oscar asked. "One for the boys? One for you two?"

"No. One for us. One for them," she said.

Oscar and Cat-Suited Woman were all over each other on the way to the rooms. Good for him, Ed thought. He tried to conjure the memory of the warmth of the sexy cop's skin but couldn't get the image of the glass shard in her husband's face from his mind. No way he was going back in over him.

"This way," Miss Sugar Skull said.

The walls were thin. Ed sat next to her on the bed and listened to his brother and her sister laughing and doing shots of something.

"What was she like? Your Francisca?" she said.

"What?"

"Your wife. Your ex-wife."

"You mean my dead wife."

"She *thinks* she's your ex-wife."

Ed remembered the sting. The slap of her hand across his face. Her wedding ring drawing blood. Making the cut that left the scar on the side of his jaw.

"We never got the divorce. We were going to. When it all went down," Ed said, then paused.

They listened to the laughter from the other room.

"How do you know what she thinks?" Ed asked.

"Doesn't matter. When what went down?"

"The last job. Listen. I'm happy Oscar's making time with your sister, but I don't want any trouble. I just need to get back home before my P.O. knows I'm gone. Okay?"

"You know what today is?"

"Day after Halloween? Day of the Dead?"

"That mean anything to you?"

"No. Should it?"

"Does your wife mean anything to you?"

Ed thought he was going to say just how much she did but he found he couldn't speak. He felt his arms close around Francisca's waist. The familiar thrum of his bike as she gunned it. And everything went blurry, then black. The loss of blood. The alcohol. How it was she who got them home that first wild night together.

"I don't talk about me. What about you? You have an old man?"

"No."

"No? Pretty girl like you. Smart. Tough. Why not?"

"My sister and I have...a gift. Life can be a burden when you're special."

A round of laughter and voices broke out next door. Were there more people in there? Some pop song kicked in. The wall vibrated with bass. Were they starting another party?

"Never met a man strong enough," Miss Sugar Skull said.

She opened her bag and took out a T-shirt and jeans and moved to the area with the mirror and sink. She ran the faucet and wiped her face. Black-and-white makeup smeared to gray. She lifted off her skull-bones top, wriggled out of her skirt, and changed clothes.

"Oh and you think I'm strong enough?" Ed asked.

"No. I'm not here to party or find a man. My sister. That's why she's here. She's seen too much and doesn't think straight anymore."

Someone pounded on the door of Oscar's room.

"Turn it down, or else," the old man from the office said.

"Fuck," Ed said. "Oscar's going to be the death of me."

"No, he's not. But it's time to leave."

"Now?"

"Come on, let's go."

"We're never going to get them to come now."

"Never was about them. It's about you. And *her*."

The music lowered.

"One more time and I'm calling the cops," the old man said.

Right here was where he knew his brother wanted to be. But he knew *he* needed to get the hell out of here. Ed opened the door and saw the old man ambling back to the office. Miss Sugar Skull took his hand and they darted to the car. She got behind the wheel. Ed felt lightheaded and the back of his arm itched. He saw more costumed people dancing on the side of the road, but when he glanced back they were gone.

"You're going east," he said.

"I know."

"Come on. You know I have to get home. Take it west."

"You've got something to do first."

"You're gonna get me arrested. What?"

"Take off your costume."

"Ah, come on," Ed said.

He let her drive. The white lines blurred into one long streak as they accelerated. He could open the door. Roll out. But would she call the cops? He still could make it home in time if they hurried through whatever she had in mind. Wherever she was taking him.

"Now's the time you tell me about her," she said.

"I said I don't talk about me."

"Talk."

Ed kept silent for a few minutes but as the miles rolled on he found himself speaking.

"I was done. Done with the life. I had a job. A good one. I was a mechanic at the garage with Mickey Samuels, a guy I went to high school with. It wasn't a union job but it was good pay. And I had weekends off.

"Then her mother went downhill. Started losing it. Lost her job. Lost her place. Moved in with us. Fran started taking care of her. To the point she lost her job too. Then I was paying for everyone. We were barely making it. Then I, *we*, decided to do one last job. And then I'd be out.

"Mickey knew of a cross-country shipment. Twenty cars. Most of them new. Nothing fancy. He was going to have them chopped for parts. Our cut would be ten grand. All we had to do was get the driver out of the way and drive the truck two miles. Two miles to the shop. It was closer but the route avoided a red- light camera and a main street with a couple of security cams. It was supposed to be easy. Knock him out at the rest stop Mickey said the guy always stopped at.

"But the guy fought back. Pushed her. Middle of the night. A car was coming too fast off the on-ramp. She got hit. Never woke up. Her mom pulled the plug two weeks later. My grand larceny charge was upped to manslaughter. For that I got three years. Three years."

Three years and I never told anyone, Ed thought. How the hell did she just get me to talk?

"There. I told you. You're so quiet. Nothing to say?"

"No," Miss Sugar Skull answered.

"Damn you're cold."

"Gotta be."

"You left them without a car."

"My sister's resourceful. She'll get by. They have nowhere they have to be. It's you that has to get home."

"So we *are* going home?"

"No. You know that. Tonight we're going somewhere else."

4. Returning to the Scene of the Crime

"The California border's west and you're taking me east," Ed said. "I'm gonna run out of time."

"You know where we're going yet?" Miss Sugar Skull asked.

"You're not listening to me, are you?" Ed said.

They passed a sign for a rest stop and it dawned on Ed.

"I'm not going there. No way," he said.

"Or what?" Miss Sugar Skull asked.

"Nothing, forget it," Ed said.

He shifted his weight. Grabbed the wheel with his left hand, grabbed her hand with his right, fast, as if it held a prison shank coming for him. He pulled hard expecting to turn the car around. The wheel didn't budge. He squeezed her hand harder.

"Turn it around," he said. "Now. Don't make this hard."

He couldn't move her hand either. She turned her head. Slow. Cool as could be. Licked her lips. He thought her expression might be a smile. Or maybe hiding that she tasted something sour.

"No," she said.

"Fuck this," Ed said.

He didn't know what her expression meant, but it unnerved him worse than anything he'd ever seen inside. He let go of her hand. Let go of the wheel. He reached for the door and found the handle. He squeezed and shouldered it. It opened. He shifted right and rolled himself out.

He hit the soft sand on the side of the road and kept on rolling. He tasted dirt. He spread out his arms. His legs. Stopped his forward motion and found his way to his knees. Then stood. And staggered. West. Maybe he couldn't make it home by morning, but he could at least cross the state line.

The Charger skidded to a halt and swung around in front of him.

Ed told himself there was no way he was getting back in. No way she was going to get him arrested. But he found himself walking toward the car. The passenger door opened. He walked over and sat inside against his will. Miss Sugar Skull watched him emotionlessly.

"I know I can't stop you," Ed said. "I wish you wouldn't do this."

"It has to be tonight. You and I both know that."

"I don't want to."

"Tell me about your Francisca."

They drove in silence. Ed rubbed his arm. The bites were raised and the area surrounding them painful.

"Once her mom moved in, things got rough. She'd drink. Get angry. Argue with me for no reason. Even when she didn't drink she'd be angry. Our arguments turned to fights. More often than not she'd hit me."

"You're a big guy. You took that?"

"It's not about size or strength. It's about the person you love. Flip side of that love. Hating you so much to strike you. I thought I deserved it. I thought I wasn't good enough. Fucked-up I know."

"But you were together for that last job."

"I never should have took her. I'd never hurt her. But she asked to come along. To make sure I didn't back out. I should have said no. But I let her come along, anyway. Part of me knew it was my way out. I knew we were over."

"You have to talk to her one more time."

"How do you know?"

"My sister and I were out on the strip yesterday afternoon."

"You live in Vegas?"

"No. We don't live anywhere. But we were...drawn. To the strip."

"Drawn?"

"Like hearing a call. This time it was your wife calling us."

"My wife? My ex-wife? My dead wife?"

"She told me you'd gotten out and your brother was taking you to the Flamingo to help you move on."

"My wife? Really?"

"She's here right now. You'll see her soon."

"Soon?"

"You don't have a lot of time."

"I'll make it. I'll be back before my P.O. knows I jumped the state. You just have to turn around and head west."

"No. The bite. I know."

She licked her lips as a desert creature would.

A procession of costumed people walking along the shoulder of the highway caught Ed's attention. Dozens of people in a straight line. All wearing sugar-skull makeup. The colors brightened the earthy tones of the desert night. Ed thought he could see the cacti through them, but when he blinked they were gone.

"It's just a bite. I'm fine."

"No. You're not."

Miss Sugar Skull drove onto the off-ramp for the rest stop.

"There's something you have to do," she said. "Take off your costume."

"You keep saying that. I'm *not* wearing one."

Miss Sugar Skull pulled the Charger into a spot. The rest stop lot was empty and just as Ed remembered. Desert sand and cacti lined the parking area beneath the huge sign that needed its bulbs changed. Processions of skull-faced people circled the lot. Groups and groups of them. Side by side. And in lines. They half-walked, half-danced to music Ed could not hear.

"What's with all the costumes?" Ed asked.

"What do you think?"

Ed shrugged.

"Helps us celebrate," she said. "Feel part of something. Honor the dead. None of that makes sense to you?"

"You took yours off back at the motel. Why?"

"I wasn't wearing a costume," she said.

Then Ed saw Francisca.

5. Forgetting Yourself

The processions merged and formed one crowd of dozens and dozens of people all surrounding her. Their colors were so bright. Vibrant. In sharp focus. The rest stop. Everything seemed blurry. Except for Francisca.

She was a vision of how she was in life. Tall. Thin. Rugged. Beautiful. All the pain of missing her retuned and filled Ed's bones. He thought he would fall down. Her lips pursed. Her face a mask of stoicism. Like she was just before they would have a fight. Like she was at the end.

Ed expected her expression to turn to rage.

"Eduardo," Francisca said. "Look at you. I'm so sorry."

"Sorry? Sorry for what? I'm sorry about you," Ed said.

Ed wanted her to say she was sorry that we went wrong. Sorry for hitting you. Sorry for everything. For our whole lives not working out the way we knew it could have.

"I'm sorry you look terrible. Poison has spread through you."

"Poison? The lizard? The bite?"

"No. A poison much, much worse. Your soul is poisoned. You've forgotten yourself."

"So I'm going to be with you?"

"No. Once you die, you're gone."

"Then why...how are you here?"

Ed turned to Miss Sugar Skull.

"I know," he said. "I get it now. You're here to tell me she's holding on to me or something. Right?"

"No," Miss Sugar Skull said.

"I forgave you long ago," Francisca said. "Today is the day I am here. The day we are here. To dance. I am sorry about us though."

"I'm sorry too, Fran. I never wanted it to end like that. I never wanted it to end at all."

Eduardo dropped to his knees. He tried to lift himself but he fell forward on his hands. All the painted faces gazed upon him.

"So we forgive each other," Ed said. "We worked it out. We get to be together now?"

"That's not how it works," Francisca said.

She disappeared. The procession moved. Step after step the skull-faced figures marched into the shadows of the cacti.

Miss Sugar Skull walked to the Charger.

"Where are you going?" Ed asked.

"To party with your brother and my sister. Maybe get a good night's sleep before the next one of you comes calling."

"Please don't leave me here."

"Here was where you were meant to go. You did what you had to do."

"She said once you die you're gone. Is that true?"

"What do you think?"

"I want to know who they all are. All the people."

"Don't know. Other than that the walls are thin today. The lines blur today. But the time for that is almost gone."

Miss Sugar Skull closed the car door and drove back to the road.

Ed thought about how he'd said after his release he'd go see his mom. He said he'd get a job. Go back to the straight and narrow.

He'd said a lot of things that he never made happen.

A skeleton-faced figure moved in the shadows. It reached a bony hand toward him.

"May I have this dance?" it said.

Ed heard himself say, "I don't dance."

He saw himself taking the bony hand. Letting himself dance along with them all into the night. He knew he was very sick. He might die here on the asphalt.

"Save me," Ed yelled to Miss Sugar Skull's departing car.

She screeched to a halt and leaned out the window.

"The most common way to get arrested is to forget yourself," Miss Sugar Skull yelled over the hum of the motor. "Better hope a cop finds you in time."

The skeleton's hand reached for him.

"Dance with us," it said. "Are you coming?"

"I don't dance," Ed said, out loud this time.

But dancing with the figures in the shadows seemed like the most natural thing to do, and he yearned to move to the music of the night sounds. He wasn't ready to take off his costume, but wasn't sure how much longer he could hold on.

RED LIGHTS

Four men come in and I call dibs on the one that hesitates and looks around nervously. The alpha male among them plants himself on the barstool next to Tanya. Her black dress, slit up the sides, shows off her long legs.

It's still early. I call the rest of the girls down, turn the music up, and dim the lights on the little stage in front of the dance floor. The power flickers then all goes dark. Red light emits from the walls, the pulsing glow caught in the martini glasses and chrome dancing pole before the lights return. The spirits are restless tonight.

The men order drinks. Two beers. One vodka. And a club soda for the one I've got my eye on. I walk over with two other girls. One of *us* for each of *them*. Mine is cute, in a puppy-dog sort of way. I put my hand on his shoulder and look him straight in the eye. He looks away.

"What's your name?" I ask, followed by a string of mundane questions to get him talking and make him feel at ease.

The girls are asking the same questions, creating the illusion of intimacy and interest.

"First time in Zurich? How long you here? Oh, what kind of business? Do you like my dress tonight?"

The alpha male has already dispensed with the pleasantries and gotten to the menu. Right to the private room and the items at the bottom of the list for him.

Puppy Dog isn't talking but when I ask, "Where are you from?" he turns the tables on me.

"Where are you from?" he asks.

"Ukraine," I say. A lie, but it matches the accent I have chosen.

"You miss it there?" he asks.

"Home?"

"Yeah, home."

"Yes. Very much," I say, astonished to find myself speaking something close to truth.

"And that's why you work."

"Yes," I say.

"How did—"

"You can say it," I say. "How did a nice girl like me end up here?"

Girls wait along the wall and at the bar for more men to enter.

"A wicked man brought me here, against my will, a long, long time ago," I say. "When he realized I would never love him and never serve him, I was forced to go to work."

"Why don't you turn him in? Or just leave?" he asks.

"Oh, he met his end, but he was strong, very strong, and his influence remains. I cannot leave until his conditions are met."

"What an ass. What the hell was wrong with him?"

"For one thing he did not believe that good men come to places like this," I say.

"We try not to," he says.

I know.

"Would you like to have a drink with me?" I ask, steering the conversation back to where I need it to go.

I can't see the red lights but I feel them flickering in alarm.

He says he's never been to a place like this before. He's just along for the ride with the guys. Here on business.

"So let's have a drink or we could..." I reach for the menu.

"So sorry...," he says.

He looks at the cut of my dress. A long look, drinking me in. Then, for the first time, he looks me straight in the eye.

"...you are...truly wonderful. But I really can't. I know time is money and I don't want to take up any more of yours."

He means it. Tonight is my lucky night.

Alpha Male and Tanya have gone upstairs. The other two men are discussing the menu. They are worthless to me. Virtueless.

Puppy Dog is cut from a different cloth. Sincere. Honest. A rare fish. Just what I need.

He tells his friend he will wait outside. I put on a sad face and let him go. After a few minutes I follow him out. Dark has come and the district has come alive. The sidewalks are busy with those looking for a bar, for a score, for a start to the night's debauchery and escape, for a place to taste the evening's first poison. Puppy Dog is standing on the sidewalk having a cigarette.

"Can I join you?" I ask.

Before he can protest I say, "I'm not working now."

"Really?" he asks.

"Just having a cigarette. With you."

We smoke and watch the street rabble. Two drug dealers squabble on the corner. Couples and drunk packs of friends in nighttime finery walk by in varying states of intoxication. The night smells of French cologne, clove cigarettes, hash. The cobblestone is bathed in streetlight, spilled beer, and soon-to-be-forgotten, too-loud laughter.

"So what is it, you gay?" I ask him.

"No."

"Ah, married. A girlfriend?"

"No. Not anymore."

"A broken heart, then?"

"I guess you could say that."

I lean in and kiss him on the cheek. My lower lip brushes the corner of his mouth. I linger. He doesn't pull away.

"Consider that my get-well wishes then," I say.

The front wall of the club is glowing red. I move to block his line of sight.

"That felt very nice," I say.

"Uh, huh," he says.

"Okay. I know how to fix this," I say. "Let *me* pay *you*."

"For what? You're crazy."

I take his hand. "Let's walk."

"Where?" he asks.

"For coffee? Chocolate?" I say.

"Ooh, I like the way you say cho-co-lat," he says. "I'd be happy to go with you. You don't have to buy a date with me."

I laugh. "I know. But *I* want to *buy* you."

"Now that's a role reversal," he says.

I take a thousand franc bill out of my pocket and playfully try to stuff it in his hand.

"No," he says and twists and squirms.

"Ten thousand then."

"No," he says. He's too strong. I can't make him take the bill.

I take out a shiny five-franc piece. "Just this, then."

I flip the coin to him. He catches it; twirls it in his fingers and puts it in his pocket.

"All right," he says. "Some hot cho-co-lat to seal the deal then."

"My flat is just this way."

"Your flat?"

"I make the best hot chocolate in town."

We walk hand in hand through the narrow, winding streets. We pass a church of stone and glass, a café—its little outside tables full of patrons drinking beer and absinthe—an artist space called the gallery of seraphim. Next to the gallery is my door. We enter. Go upstairs to my small room.

An elegant glass bottle and a single candle sit on my table.

I light the candle and kiss him. He does not resist. I tug his shirt from his pants.

"Oh, no," he says.

"Yes. I bought you."

He hesitates. Even overcome with desire his morality controls him. A rare fish indeed.

"I want you," I say. "You. I told you I'm not working."

And I am not. I am filled with desire. A desire to go home again. And he is helping me.

"Don't you want to fuck me?"

His resistance gone, he comes to me. We wriggle out of our clothes. He's clumsy. Our teeth clack. His trousers are stuck around his ankles.

I pull him closer. Take him in my hand. And guide him into me.

With his climax, there is a puff of sulfur and his body goes slack. The room goes dark and a red glow appears in the bottle on the table. I roll his empty shell off me. It falls lifeless to the floor. I stopper the bottle. Seal it with candle wax.

I take the bottle back to the cabaret. The night crowd has rolled in. Alpha Male and one of the other men are still in the upstairs rooms. The third is spending his cash on stage dances.

I go behind the bar and into the back room. I open the hidden panel only my hands can open. Inside the hidden space are bottles. Vintage, elegant bottles. All of them glow red, like the one in my hand.

I place the bottle with Puppy Dog's soul in it on the shelf and kiss it.

"Yes, Puppy Dog. I want to go home. And I have so many more to collect before I am able. It has been a very good year, but even at this pace I have still a century or two to go."

I kiss the bottle, close the panel, and head back into the sea of human flotsam for more hunting.

THE CANOPY CRAWLERS

We soar above the living green canopy; rotors flitting like the agile dragonfly wings that inspired them. The jungle's time of need had come. That's what Presidente Marquez had said, in her speech summoning the reserves to active duty. The enemy had arrived not only from somewhere in space, but surfaced from deep in the earth and the forest floors.

Times are strange, old rivals allying, like us and the Colombians, while other nations seize the opportunity to fight, hoping for some stupid, meaningless advantage as everything goes to hell. Me, I'd just as soon see the rest of the world burn, but I fight, *we* fight for the forest. The demons can have the cities, those concrete wastelands, for whatever it is they want, but my squad will defend the trees to the last.

"Look sharp," my patrol-mate Juanita says, her voice tinny in my helmet's fitted earpiece.

She dives even closer to the trees, the emerald-painted top of her sleek Aztec-140 blending into the sea of leaves. She silently passes through a cloud of blue butterflies. The sparkling insects disperse, swirling in her invisible wake. I follow, without question, and pull the throttle to match her dive.

"That's not it," she says out loud, to herself, not me. Two weeks and I'm used to her already.

Juanita's got senses. She just knows things, before they're going to happen and all. Nothing so developed to be picked up by the bureau, I don't think. But she's one of the longest to survive out here, and you've got to be special for that. I heard in the mess that only one guy, Pedro or Pietro from the Nighthawk Air Rangers, has flown more. That's got to be the luck of a crazy fool. You've got to be crazy flying near-surface scouting, almost blind. I'm still sane enough to know how lucky I am to be partnered with Juanita and scared enough to remember to ask the Lord to let me survive.

Juanita banks her plastic-alloyed Aztec, spins and rolls, flashing its sky blue bottom. Her rotors come together Y-like, almost flapping, changing the flow of air. She shoots up, perfectly vertical, and races off at seven o'clock. If any other Crawler pulled such a stunt I'd rail her for showboating, but there's no one here but us and the jungle. And whatever Juanita senses.

Last night in the heliport, as we headed back to the bunks after checking our blades, I asked her why our squad is called the

Canopy Crawlers. She looked at me like I was stupid, then glided her hand in front of her like a plane and whistled.

"Gotta protect the trees."

Probably some throwback to some Mayan shit or banana republic term, but I knew the Canopy Crawlers was also the name of the ghosts supposedly protecting the forest with us.

"We get the name 'cause we're the best," she said.

I believed we were the best and I believed in the ghosts too.

"When a tree goes bad, it goes bad," she continued, shaking her head. "When it turns it'll eat a hundred just like that."

I wanted her to talk more but from the sour look on her face I knew she was done.

I couldn't imagine how something could eat a single tree, let alone a hundred. Maybe she was crazy. Maybe she'd spent too much time in the treetops like that guy from the Rangers. I've never actually seen a tree turn, though I saw the briefing vids of the North Petén, right after the first attack. A smoldering mass of sticky tar, right in the middle of the Mayan Biosphere Preserve, where a thousand acres of pristine rainforest used to be.

Juanita was there. She saw what the ancient hardwood in the center had become. It would have eaten the whole rainforest if the ghosts, the real Canopy Crawlers, our namesakes, hadn't come.

"I'm feeling something, Ramon," Juanita says. "Twelve clicks from here. Outside Copán."

I already knew she felt something and was zeroing in, just by following her erratic flight.

136

"Arm your harmonics."

I was hoping she wouldn't say that. That meant a tree was going to turn. Central Command had just fitted our Aztecs with sonics and I'd never used them before. They fire a focused burst of sound that, for some reason, stuns the turned trees. Another trick they learned from the ghosts "that don't exist," I bet.

I don't trust Command. How can I? Officially, they say the Canopy Crawlers don't exist. But all of the brass I know believes in the ghosts too. When I asked Juanita for her thoughts, she told me they are the spirits of ancient Mayan rulers given flesh by the will of the jungle. I believed her. Then she laughed, but it seemed as good an answer as any. Less strange than the things they call demons eradicating the cities.

I look at the weapons display glowing on the inside of the windscreen, and arm my sonics. I picture the three square slats, like gills on each side of my Aztec's long sleek tail opening. I swallow and try to pop my ears as my helmet's protective cups lock around them.

My screen's sensors go hot. Thousands of red blips, most tiny, some larger, moving away from a point in the center. Central Command doesn't know when or what tree is going to turn. But the animals know and they always run, about two minutes before. Someone in Command got smart and rigged a network of motion sensors to pick up any erratic animal movements. A perfect warning.

I descend as close as I can to the treetops, following Juanita as she races to the tree that's going to go bad. A family of howler monkeys swing from the upper branches, mouths open in screams. I hear nothing but see their teeth and hear the remembered sound in my head. A tree full of macaws takes to the air in a cloud of red. Juanita maneuvers nimbly and doesn't shred a feather.

"Patrol nine," Central Command says in my ear. "Motion grid is picking up a mass exodus. Quadrant three, sector five-two-oh. Repeat: sector five-two-oh."

I picture Juanita's disdain as she hears the announcement.

"We're already on it," I answer. "Clock reads fifty-five seconds."

"Fifteen seconds till," Juanita says to me.

I knew better than to ask her if she was sure, but the clock said fifty seconds till turning.

"This one's different," she says. "It's going to be big."

I see the top of the ancient Mayan temple on the horizon. Colors flare above, the friction on hulls in the sky. An attack from space too? What do they want here? The temple? The jungle-covered city? Perhaps any city is the same to them, even if it has been abandoned for a thousand years.

"Enemy presence confirmed in low atmosphere," Command says.

I don't ask if they are sending the fleet to counter and defend. They better. But I know we are stretched as thin as can be.

We reach the center of the grid and hover. I notice shimmering areas above the canopy—like mirages, hard to see. Three blurry patches of air ripple above a big, old strangler fig.

"That strangler, that's it," Juanita says.

My counter reads thirty-seven...thirty-six...Juanita counts...three...two...

Before I can ask about the shimmering, the tree expels its leaves, like in the vid, stripping itself of anything green in a spray of vines and creepers. Its rich brown bark darkens to black. Limbs stretch and grow like monstrous arms and claws. Something about it exudes sickness and my stomach drops. The leaves shrivel and blacken as they fall to the ground. The enemy has taken the tree.

"Here we go!" Juanita says, and dives into the mess of growing branches. Blackened tentacles shoot in all directions from the bare limbs, then snake for her.

She uses her Aztec's rotors to shear off branches and tentacles. New ones sprout where the old are cut. Dirt sprays as a wriggling mass of roots burst from the ground. The demon tree lumbers out of the hole where it once stood, reaching for the surrounding forest.

Wherever they are touched, trees shrivel and fall like decaying leaves in fast motion. Not even a minute and Juanita is like a silver fly in a blackened crater.

"Back up here!" Juanita screams in my ear.

I realize I have been watching, transfixed like a rookie. Juanita makes the cuts and goes for the kill, without the backup of my sonics. I watch branches and tendrils reach in the air fractions of seconds behind her.

I fire two sonic arrows hoping to buy time. I feel pressure in my ears but hear nothing. The tree thing stops like a vid frame on freeze. Its branches and tentacles stop growing and reaching. It quivers all over, thick trunk pulsing, twisted boughs shaking—like a vibrating speaker about to blow.

Juanita spins, continuing her evasive rolls as if the branches were still reaching for her. If I hadn't fired maybe they would have grabbed her. She pulls up and circles the giant husk.

I glance up. White and faint yellow coronas glow around the distant specks in the sky. The spacecraft have entered the low atmosphere. Colors flash against the sky blue. A firefight. Probably the Seventh Fleet defending.

I shift my jaw as my protective gear slides from my ears.

"Looks like we made it," I say to Juanita. She makes another pass around the tree, shearing off a blackened bough. "Let's get out of here before that battle in the sky touches down."

"Not a chance. Get over here and help me shred this rotten weed." She knows I am afraid. Afraid to get close. She's never said a thing, but she knows. She's good enough to fly inside, make the kill, and let me back her up. But now, when it is safer, she brings me in. I know she wants me to finish this one. For my sake.

The tree shakes violently and its blackened bark flies off with a pop. Fresh tendrils reach for us. I pull up. I feel something clip my tail, but I make it above the canopy out of reach.

I turn to see Juanita's Aztec going down. Just like that. One hit. From the best there ever was, to fragile and spinning. She crashes through low branches and skids to a stop on the mulchy forest floor. Her Aztec crumpled and smoking.

The tree reaches for me. I pull up higher. My Aztec whines. I'll have to go back and land soon or face this thing alone.

Below, three insect-like shapes materialize out of the shimmering places above the canopy. They float motionless, except for the blue of the sky and the green of the leaves swirling on their surface as if liquid mercury. The shapes solidify into giant dragonfly-things with reflective skin. Shiny and metallic. Full of seashell-mica colors. Mandibles open, compound eyes rotate, mantis arms unfold and extend—each hooked barb glittering in the sun.

I knew the Canopy Crawlers were real. I hope I survive to tell. This battle is going to be fierce if they showed up here. An insistent buzzing reaches my ears despite my helmet's protection. I remember the kind face of my dad. One day after his work on the chicle tree plantations he held a cicada by one wing and pointed to its wriggling legs. The world is full of sound, he told me. These little things make some of the loudest noises you'll ever hear. I realize I'm transfixed again, staring at the colors reflecting in the Crawlers' skin. I need to focus if I'm going to stay alive.

I don't know how the Crawlers make the buzzing sound, but I know it comes from them. They roll toward the tree, a flight path like Juanita's, like Juanita idealized that is, their motion perfect—a speed and precision of movement no Aztec could ever match.

The tree forgets about me and lurches toward them. My Aztec thrumming, I bank around to get below the canopy and find

Juanita.

I manage a shaky touchdown. The tree about fifty yards behind me; the sound of falling trees around it audible somewhere beneath the grating, yet strangely melodic buzz. The three Canopy Crawlers fly circles around its trunk. They quicken, taking more intricate flight paths, in between and around branches. I can only see them as a blur—a silver-blue blur.

I take one last look at Juanita's position on my sensors and open my cockpit. My tail rotor is corroded and decaying where one of those tentacles grazed it.

Over my shoulder I see the towering hulk of the tree teetering, about to fall, surrounded by an electric cloud—the Crawlers, circling too fast for me to see.

I run toward Juanita. The ground shakes with a huge boom. I turn again, but the tree is still standing. A cloud of smoke wafts from the trees. A downed ship.

Through the spaces in the canopy I see the sky full of the colors of hundreds of ships entering the atmosphere. The fight is going to be here soon, wrecking this place with the crossfire of lasers, energy weapons, and the demon's strange munitions.

Juanita's Aztec is close by, up against a mound of dirt the jungle has grown over—a section of ancient bricks interlaced with tree roots, exposed by the crash.

The tail is bent over, the rotors twisted, but her cockpit is open. She either ejected or crawled out. A few drops of blood lead into the jungle. A line of leafcutter ants march in the same direction, away from the fighting. I follow and come upon Juanita on her hands and knees. Besides the open gash on her forearm she doesn't look too bad. She can't be that bad, she's talking to herself.

"Come on, wrong way," I say to her. "We're getting out of here. The Crawlers finished that thing, but I think more are coming."

I point to the line of fleeing leafcutters.

Juanita makes a gagging sound then a click from her throat. I run to stop her from choking.

"Stay back!" she says, forceful enough to stop me in my tracks, then makes more throaty clicks.

"Let him see. He has a future," she says to herself.

The air around her begins to shimmer. I look over my shoulder—the turned tree is no longer standing, the blue cloud of Crawlers gone.

The shimmering air ripples and the three Canopy Crawlers materialize around her. The jungle is silent. I have never heard it so quiet. No buzz. Not a single chirping frog or cackling bird; only the soft clicking of the Canopy Crawlers, big as Aztecs, moving around Juanita. They touch and probe her cuts with the slender pointed tips of their mantis arms. I lurch forward.

"It's okay," she says, a pained look on her face I've never seen before.

If they hurt her I'll kill them. I take another step forward.

The Crawler closest to me rotates its big bug head toward me. I see my reflection in its compound eyes. Its mandibles open and close, its gaze silent and sentient, as if considering whether to maul me. I wouldn't believe my eyes, but the line of leafcutter ants circle around the pointed tip of its leg in the jungle floor and continue on their way.

The Crawler turns back to Juanita. The others each balance two silvery blue spheres on the pointed tips of their arms. Secretions of some kind? They look liquid and jiggle slightly as the Crawlers lower them to Juanita's eyes, nose, and the gash on her arm.

The spheres ooze into her eyes and nostrils as if being sucked in. The one on her cut spreads, coating her arm in a silvery-blue sheen and flows up her shoulder and down her chest.

I run to her, not caring if I get mauled. The Crawlers ignore me. I grab her wrist, the one not coated in the spreading stuff. Her pulse is almost gone. I move my face close to hers. I want to tell her she was the best there ever was, but she wouldn't want that, so I ask about the war.

"What do you mean I have a future? Do we win? Have you seen?"

I want to hear something like, you'll become the best pilot ever, or, we win the war and the forests return to cover the earth.

She makes clicking sounds. I move my hand away as the blue droplet spreads over her wrist. She leans her head to me. Her eyes are silver and laced with diamond-like facets. We don't touch, but somehow I can feel her muscles relaxing and sense her lungs and heart slowing.

She opens her mouth. She moves so close, if I didn't know better I'd think she was trying to kiss me.

"Gotta defend the trees," she manages to say, then the blue oozes up her neck and covers her face. For a second I see the shape of her Mayan nose underneath and then a formless nothing. Her coated hand reaches up and grabs me, tight. I feel myself shake, like from an electric shock, but no pain. I think I'm feeling her die, the electricity leaving her—her mind and her muscles powering down. Clicks and buzzes ring in my mind. I stagger backward into the Crawler behind me. I turn. It rotates its head and looks at me inquisitively. Then the clicking sounds subside. I know Juanita is gone.

The jungle is quiet but I can sense all the fleeing animals and the Crawlers around me. Farther out in the jungle I sense a presence. A sense of wrong blooms in my gut akin to that sick sensation of knowing a bad cold is about to hit.

I reach for the presence and hone in on a tree. No, twelve trees. Twelve trees are going to turn; I know this as certain as I know my hands are attached to my arms. This sensation is what Juanita felt, how she knew.

One of the Crawlers takes her cocooned form in its mantis arms. Another turns to me and makes that clicking noise. Somehow I understand it is telling me she will return and see me again in battle.

They shimmer and disappear in a rippling patch of air. A second later I hear their buzz, their battle cry, from above.

I run to my Aztec and ascend above the canopy.

The sky above the temple is full of hundreds of ships, tiny black specks from this distance, but I know they are huge. My screen shows the rest of my squad and the Nighthawks converging on the position.

I bark information to Central Command. "Be advised, a dozen trees will turn in sector five-oh in...less than one minute. Forces passing through be on alert and ready to respond."

"Patrol nine," Command responds. "Verify this information."

I ignore them. I race toward a big hardwood about to turn. I see the Nighthawks approaching, in a wedge-like battle formation. I can feel them, sense their presence, and the presence of a dozen Crawlers flying above them, invisible and undetected.

My helmet locks over my ears. I'm afraid. I wish Juanita was here. Maybe I'll see her again, a shimmering blue ghost above the canopy. But for now, I gotta protect the trees.

THE WISH MECHANICS

*...and with the grace
of the Motherland's kisses,
all your dreams will be made true
by the Ministry of Wishes.*

—Union of Civilized Countries,
Official Nursery Rhyme

Allie fixed pipes for Local 42, big government contract stuff; though for her whole life she had wanted to design. Her red pipe wrench gripped the shining metal pipe like an arm-sized lobster claw and she pulled. Her partner, Big Mike, slathered the joint with sticky blue pipe-dope. The gelatinous cream spread across the seam, turned clear, and started to harden. Allie neatened it with her trowel. "That'll hold her," she said, pushing her dirty blonde hair off her grease-streaked face. She wiped her hands on her coveralls, smiling at the neat angles of pipes filling the cavernous under-basement of the Plaza of Ministries. They were insulated, wrapped and clearly labeled, "blue" for supply, "red" for return. The check valves and emergency cutoff switches were easily accessible.

Mike checked the prints. "We're done," he said, the unwieldy documents seemed almost the right size next to his girth. "And two hours early. You must've saved a hundred feet of pipe."

Allie knew she had a gift. Still, she wished someone other than Mike recognized it.

They gathered their wrenches and ratchets and put them in their weathered gray tool chest. Allie picked up their trash from lunch, activated the chest's hover mechanism, and together they guided the four-foot long, floating box through the maze of colored pipes and whirring machinery toward the service lift.

The noiseless lift stopped and let them out at the Plaza's main service entrance, spacious and open, not like the basement that powered it. The Union of Civilized Countries insignia hung above the tunnel leading to the elevators. Light seemed to come from everywhere, for there were no shadows, not even by the banks of time-card machines.

Hundreds of blue-uniformed maintenance workers filled the chamber. Allie brushed off her coveralls and tried to neaten her hair as she walked in. The workers held up their time chip cards to be scanned, most clipped to pockets or on chains around their necks, as they walked past the bank of time clock terminals. Allie thought of her husband Simon, at home in the small apartment they shared. Since the job was done early she had more time to spend with him, more time to try to shake him from his never-ending depression.

Allie was reaching for her job chip when the alarm sounded.

"Unauthorized personnel," a metallic voice boomed over a blaring siren. "This is not a warning."

Workers rushed to the walls and dropped to the floor. Two men scrambled past the clock terminals toward the doors leading out of the building. The intruders. They were dressed as mechanics.

Two black circles the size of large flowerpots, the bottom of security tubes, appeared on the ceiling. With a hydraulic hiss, the tubes lowered from the ceiling, exposing man-sized cylinders of black metal. Enforcers, Allie thought. Something bad must be happening.

The tubes burst and the enforcers unfolded their thin arms like spiders leaving their hiding places to hunt. The pair of spindly, insect-like robots leapt to the ground, the tips of their tapered legs clicking on the floor.

The intruders dashed for the doors. Red laser dots from the enforcers' basketball-sized bodies marked them. Mike tugged on Allie's coveralls. "Come on, get down," he said.

"Stop!" one of the intruders yelled. "There is another way, the world can be so much different if we all just believed."

Blue-white bolts of electricity arced from the enforcers to the fleeing man with a crackle, like a control panel shorting out. He flopped to the ground, a small puff of blue-gray smoke rising from his twitching body.

The two spidery robots surrounded the lone intruder. He jagged right, then left trying to get around them, but he was trapped; a pointy arm in his way no matter which way he tried to run.

The siren stopped and the crowd of workers got up and went about their business as if nothing happened. Allie stole another look. A small arc of electricity jumped from the fallen body to the floor before dissipating.

"Damn Raven Guild," Mike said. "Cowardly saboteurs. Never satisfied with what we got." He shook his head in disdain. "More enforcers and their handlers should be here soon for them."

Allie didn't follow politics closely. She preferred to spend her days sunning on her building's roof deck, with a trade journal in her lap and her husband by her side. She knew the Guild considered the Union of Civilized Countries and its great megalopolises a blight. Simon had told her, more than once, that he dreamed of a place with real grass, a place where a man could live off the land, though he never openly supported the Guild. Allie knew that real grass only existed on the roof-domes of the inconceivably rich or in the few public nature sanctuaries. She recognized his ache for something more than his job fixing repulsion engines for the Ministry of Transportation; but nothing she did could ever fill his void.

Allie and Mike guided the chest down a ramp into the parking lot outside. Peeking out above the big green dumpsters reeking of rot and decay were the silvery towers of the skyline. The sparkling spires disappeared from view as they neared their truck parked up against the industrial-gray security barrier.

Mike pressed his hand against the truck and the back doors slid open with a soft purr. The lift gate lowered and the ramp extended like a metallic tongue to swallow the toolbox. Mike retrieved a beer from the mini cooler he had rigged into the truck's power cell and cracked it open. Allie noticed a man in the clean, green work shirt of a supervisor watching them from the next row of trucks. His boots and jeans were unstained and his tool pouch looked stiff and unused.

Allie motioned to Mike to put the beer down. The man strode over. As he stepped in the shadow of the barrier a rippling halo appeared around his head, like a heat mirage on the road. Allie rubbed her eyes and dismissed the halo as a trick of the light.

"Allie McAulife?" the man asked.

"Yeah," she said. Mike took a defensive step toward her, while trying to keep the beer out of view.

The man laughed. It reminded her of Mr. Goethels, her favorite shop teacher in the academy.

"Don't worry about the beer," the man said, in a good-natured tone. "It's a hot day. I work upstairs. I just want to have a word with your comrade here. In private."

"You want to talk to this guy?" Mike asked.

"It's okay. Go on, I'll be fine," Allie said, curious as to what the strange man had to say. If they were in trouble she'd be better able to handle it without Mike's temper.

Mike sat down on the lift gate and picked up his beer with a suspicious eye on the stranger.

"My truck is this way," the man said, gently ushering Allie away.

Allie stared at his rippling halo. When she squinted and focused, for an instant it appeared to be a circle of tiny, almost-translucent, winged lizards racing around his head.

The man noticed her staring. "Ah, I forget I have it on. Don't worry, it's a security device. How do I explain it? Let's just say it helps me keep track of things when times get rough."

Allie shrugged. She'd seen stranger things working government jobs.

The man stopped at a white truck that looked much like hers except for the emblem on its side; a simple circle around stylized clasped hands. Allie didn't recognize the symbol right away and had to recite to herself the mnemonic device from the academy for the names of the more obscure Ministries. My dog's left paw, she thought. "P" Poisons and Antidotes. "A" Antiquities and Futures. "W" Wishes. The Ministry of Wishes.

She thought the Ministry of Wishes was nothing more than a line from an old official nursery rhyme.

> *...with the grace*
> *of the Motherland's kisses,*
> *all your dreams will be made true*
> *by the Ministry of Wishes.*

The man watched her face as she mulled over the thought.

"Yes, the Ministry of Wishes is real," he said. "My name is Hector Christoffel, Operations Minister of the Ministry of Wishes. I have a job for you. That is, if you're willing."

Allie's stomach fluttered. Here, before her, was a real live minister. She spoke the first thing that came to her mind. "I already have a job, and I'm happy at it."

"Well, consider this an opportunity," Christoffel said. "You might even say an opportunity to design."

How did he know I wanted to design? Allie thought. He couldn't.

Behind Christoffel a quartet of the spider-like enforcers crawled across the lot leading the intruder they had captured inside. One of the enforcers had its spindly arm stuck into to the prisoner's neck, who now walked calm and blank-eyed. They stopped before a door in the security barrier. It slid open, revealing two shaven-headed handlers from the Ministry of Defense waiting in the tunnel through the thick wall. One handler signaled with his hand and the emotionless procession disappeared into dark.

"Ah, the Raven Guild," Christoffel said, a solemn look on his face. "Always infiltrating and planting little seeds of destruction at the ministries. Sometimes it takes weeks for us to figure out their plots within plots, but we always catch them and set things right."

Allie didn't know what he meant but said nothing so as not to appear out of touch. She wanted to know the details of this opportunity he offered.

Christoffel opened the door of his truck. "Come on," he said. "There's enough time for me to show you our facilities, I'll take you home after."

Christoffel pulled into a space around back of a small building on the outskirts of the Plaza. A small government insignia adorned the door above the words Union of Civilized Countries. Christoffel opened it and they both entered. An impossibly long hallway greeted them. Its transparent walls stretched back farther than Allie could see. Behind them were huge workrooms filled with workers attending twisting pipes and machinery. The building appeared bigger inside than it was on the outside, but Allie knew this couldn't be so. She turned to Christoffel, unsure if it had been a good idea to come.

"What kind of job is this anyway?" she asked.

"A wish mechanic," Christoffel said.

"W-what?"

"We need you to help shape the world. That's what wish mechanics do."

"Me?" Allie asked.

"You're the best at what you do. That's what counts here. If you accept you'll get to work the machines and tend the pipelines helping us spin the fabric of reality from the wishes of good citizens. Don't worry about the how and why, that's all done by the higher ups."

Allie glanced at one of the pipes. She couldn't see its source or what it fed. It scintillated pleasing shades of orange and purple and gently pulsed as if it were thin plastic and a big jet of water were passing through.

"What exactly would I have to do?" she asked.

"Chart and tend the flow of wishes. For you it'll be easy. Come on, I'll show you."

Allie felt uneasy at how Christoffel referred to wishes as things that could be piped, but the system and machinery were too fascinating not to take a closer look.

Allie followed Christoffel down the hall. He touched the clear wall and an entrance slid open. They walked down a flight of almost invisible steps into the bustling workroom.

The room buzzed with the whirs and clicks of well-oiled machinery, though Allie saw no moving parts. Christoffel took her to a young woman who had both of her hands pressed flat on a section of twelve-inch pipe.

"LaJean," Christoffel said. "I want you to meet one of our new recruits, Allie McAulife. Can you give her a demonstration of how the system works?"

"Sure," LaJean replied, "We just installed new filters. Today we're monitoring the flow rate. It's different for everyone, I either touch the pipe with my hand or touch it with my pipe wrench, you know, to get that hum."

Allie knew the hum she spoke of. She could tell if a pipe was at the correct pressure just by the metallic buzz. Could this be the same?

"And that's all there is to it—direct the wishes the super says down the pipeline and all others down toward the filters. Give it a try?"

Allie stepped away.

"These are real wishes? The hopes and dreams of real people?" she asked.

"People just like yourself," Christoffel said. "I wouldn't have brought you here if we didn't think you were qualified."

LaJean smiled at her. "This pipeline leads to the Ministry of Weather. Just let the sunny days go on past and turn anything else to the connection."

Allie gingerly placed her hands on the thrumming pipe. As she touched it images flooded her mind. The big orange sun, heat rising off concrete and steel, hundreds of different sunny days from hundreds of different perspectives.

"Good," Christoffel said. "Just let them pass into you and through you."

Images flickered in Allie's mind's eye and moved so fast until she could no longer see them and was only filled with the sensation of being in the sunshine.

"I think she's got it," LaJean said.

An image of a stormy day flowed past. Allie's knees buckled and she let go of the pipe.

"What was that?" Allie asked.

"Someone wishing for a stormy day; in July, can you believe it?" LaJean said.

"Don't worry, the filters will pick it up. That's enough for today. Thank you, LaJean," Christoffel said.

"Nice to meet you," LaJean said.

"I think you're going to work out fine," Christoffel said.

Allie smiled self-consciously.

"Come on, I mean it," Christoffel said.

Allie's smile widened.

"What do you say?"

"I'm in," Allie said.

"I knew you would be. I'll take care of the paperwork, but there are a couple of rules and important details. One: Always route the wishes in the direction you are told. It seems simple, but you'd be surprised how many old-timers here still forget this one and clog up the pipes. Two: Never touch the wish of a friend or a relative. This rarely happens. The higher ups see to it that none come your way, but should it happen it always spells trouble. And three: Always wear this."

Christoffel held out his hand revealing a translucent egg the size of a small stone.

"Hold still," he said, and stepped closer to her.

He gently tapped the stone on her head like he was breaking an eggshell. Allie heard a faint squawk, then the beating of hummingbird-fast wings buzz her ear, and then nothing.

"Security gear. Like mine," Christoffel said. "In case of a system breakdown."

Allie smiled nervously, imagining herself with a blurred halo like she had seen on Christoffel earlier.

"Welcome aboard," he said.

The rest of her first week had passed smoothly and Allie felt oriented, like an old pro. She sat on the roof of her building enjoying the Saturday afternoon sun, with a trade journal in her lap and synthetic grass between her toes. Simon sat next to her scrolling through job and real estate listings on his holographic screen that followed the movements of his face. She leaned in to give him a kiss and he jerked his head away. She wondered if he even noticed her wounded look.

"Look at this," Simon said, his voice squeaking as it did when he was frustrated. "There's a couple of open jobs repairing harvesters for the Ministry of Agriculture." He frowned. "But there's no houses or farms where we could ever afford to live. Not in a dozen lifetimes. We'd have to be in a building again. What's the use?"

Allie thought of mentioning the raise in pay that came with her new job. She thought of suggesting that they could spend her two weeks vacation at a biological reserve or the Grand Canyon hydroelectric dam, but decided against it. He always had an answer.

Allie stood and slipped into her flip-flops. She stared at Simon's sun-lit face, the shadow of his nose flickering blue and purple with reflections from the glowing listings. She darted her face forward and planted a kiss on his cheek. He didn't pull away, but his eyes never left the screen. She didn't know if he saw her gather her things and leave.

On Monday, Allie arrived at her workstation at five to nine. A holo of Christoffel spoke the daily assignment for Allie's group of mechanics.

"Today we're going to open the overflow valves and divert the flow to reservoir B while silver team installs the new piping," Christoffel's holo said.

Easy enough, Allie thought. She grabbed her pipe wrench and went off to work with her partner for the day, Richard, a wiry old man who claimed to be a librarian. He said Christoffel was an old administrator, not a job super, and claimed the big pipe wrenches he and Allie carried were portable scanners that read book catalog numbers. This seemed strange at first to Allie, but ultimately it didn't matter. It even made some strange sense, since other people she had met claimed they worked in other odd professions, such as priest, computer programmer, and interactive holograph tourist software salesman. LaJean must have been a steamfitter once too because she said she saw the system network as a series of pipes and machinery, not as a huge library needing organizing or some other place.

Allie and Richard put their lunch pails down near their assigned section of pipe, a big conduit coming from the Ministry of Time and Synchronization. Her big, red pipe wrench gripped the connection and she pulled. She felt the flow of wishes enter and pass through her. She diverted them away from the main pipeline and into the outlet leading to the reservoir. A wish passed into her that felt familiar; an image of her and Simon living on a farm with green grass and trees. She pulled back on the pipe wrench, stopping the flow.

"Hey, what's the hang up?" Richard called to her.

Allie lingered in the image. It was Simon's wish. It felt so real, but she knew she had to let it go.

"Nothing," Allie answered. "Just getting a better grip." She turned her wrench, letting the wish pass on to the reservoir with the rest of them.

That night while lying in bed with Simon sleeping next to her, Allie imagined she was living in the world she saw in his wish. He was happy, surrounded by trees and grass on a plot of his own land. She tried to get some sleep. In the morning they would be rerouting the reservoirs through the new pipes. If his wish became real, he would always be happy and she wouldn't worry about him anymore. As she drifted into sleep she envisioned routing Simon's wish through the complex mazes of pipes.

The next morning Allie opened the pipe from the reservoir and guided the wishes through the new silvery pipes. She touched every wish, waiting to feel the familiar one. With about an hour until quitting time, she felt Simon's wish again. She guided it through the main line, and easily routed it against the current around Richard, who was working farther up on the line to ensure any wish she missed went to the proper filters. She watched the pipe pulse with Simon's wish. She led it past the valves designed to sort and direct them to the furnaces of the proper ministries, or if not there to oblivion. She pushed it against the flow and in the wrong way through pipes to avoid detection by other mechanics. She watched it join the main pipe and disappear into the distance, into the outside world, where it would weave into the fibers of reality. Soon Simon's wish would be part of reality and she and Simon would live in the world of his dreams. Allie looked back at the path the wish had traveled. It was a complex series of routings; she doubted anyone would be able to track it, but to her it seemed so simple.

A few minutes before five, Allie walked up the flight of clear stairs that led into the hall where she first arrived with Christoffel. She walked through the hallway to the lone, unadorned door, opened it, and passed through. Her body tingled, like ants were racing all over her; and then her world went dark for an instant. After the flash of darkness she realized, instead of stepping from the door into the street near the Plaza, she had walked into her house, the house she and Simon had lived in, in Simon's wish. Through the big bay window she saw Simon outside on the porch, scrolling through a holo-screen. Allie ran to him.

"Hi, hon," Simon said, looking up from the screen. "I didn't see you come in."

Simon had gained some weight, in all the right places. His eyes were clear and his beard full and healthy. The porch overlooked a vibrant green backyard. Real grass, Allie thought. Not the scratchy stuff.

A small greenhouse, packed with colorful blossoms, stood next to a wooden toolshed. Simon took her hand. "I was just looking up what kind of fertilizer the clematis vines like."

Allie followed the twisting purple-blossomed vines up to the top of an old oak tree. Only a black speck high above, perhaps a plane or bird, marred the perfect blue sky.

"Come on, dinner's ready," Simon said.

Allie followed him into the house. They passed a desk covered in blueprints on the way to the kitchen.

"Mrs. Gestol called while you were out," Simon said, looking at the desk. "She said she wants to beef up the security system of her new house."

Allie realized the desk was hers and that Mrs. Gestol was one of her clients. They passed a mirror and Allie stopped to look. Her hair was lighter and longer and her waist was slimmer. She wore earrings and a low-cut flowered sundress that showed off her curves usually obscured by coveralls. Simon's world indeed, she thought.

Simon had prepared her favorite meal, roasted chicken and red potatoes. She figured there'd be no harm in eating before getting her bearings.

Simon plunked the glasses on the table. "You look terrible," he said. "Are you okay? Let me get you a drink."

Simon had never been this attentive, Allie thought as he poured her a beer. Over dinner, he was vibrant and excited. He told her stories of his thriving landscape business—he took care of an entire private community—with enthusiasm and humor.

After dinner, in the living room, Simon flicked through the news stations. Images of dark skies and burning cities whisked by before Simon clicked the holo-screen off and went to the stairs to the bedroom.

"Simon," Allie said softly. "I know this may sound strange, but you have to tell me what is going on in the world."

Simon looked at her as if she had just poured a pitcher of lemonade onto his prized flowers.

"Why do they even show that crap?" he said angrily. "Don't worry, between the wasps, the poisons, and the defense grid they'll never get in here. This house is our little island of paradise. It's all I ever wished for. As long as I have you and all this, the world can go to hell."

Apparently, it did, Allie thought as Simon stormed up the stairs.

Allie lay on the couch wondering about the world she had left behind. If it weren't for my security halo, would I not remember, she thought. She knew she had to do something, but for now all her tired mind and body could do was sleep.

Simon was already in the garden when Allie awoke the next morning.

She sleepily went in the kitchen to wake up with some orange juice. She poured a glass. It tasted sweeter, somehow cleaner than she recalled. Then she remembered that in Simon's world everything would be grown natural like the old ways. She rushed into the yard, excited to see the garden and to make more sense of the consequences of Simon's wish.

Simon was pouring a pitcher of blue fluid onto the base of his purple-blossomed clematis vine.

"See," he said, with a warm smile, "It likes acidic soil."

The lush green vine had climbed up the trellis against a ten-foot white wall that surrounded the yard. A security barrier, she thought. The clematis snaked from the trellis to an oak tree, whose trunk stretched twenty feet in the air. The yard felt different than the home she remembered. Maybe this is what it feels like to be near so many plants that are alive, she thought. She followed the trunk to where its limbs branched and reached for the sky. A black shape, like yesterday, caught her attention. This one was bigger. Closer.

"Simon!" Allie yelled. "What's that?"

Something big, like a bird or insect, held a black spidery form and something human-shaped in its grip. The mass of wings and legs soared over the house. To Allie, it looked like the wasp was carrying a wriggling enforcer robot that had been fused with a Ministry of Defense handler.

Allie took a deep breath to slow her heart. She had started to sweat.

"Don't worry, honey," Simon said, "It's just a patrol. We're close to the city but this is a good neighborhood. Still, sometimes they get in."

"Sometimes what gets in?" Allie asked.

Simon laughed and looked at her as if the monstrosity in the sky were something common.

"Come on in, I'll make you some brunch," he said, ignoring her.

"I don't want brunch," she said, raising her voice, "I want you to tell me what is going on."

Simon's mask of a smile changed. "You know damn well what was going on when you agreed to move here with me. I thought you wanted me to be happy, but no. You can't stand the thought of it."

He stormed into the house.

Back where I started, Allie thought. He's worse than ever. Maybe we're not meant to be happy together, not in any world. I have to contact Christoffel.

She went inside to her desk and tried to contact the Ministry of Wishes. As she suspected, her com-unit was useless and her holo-screen provided no information on the ministries or any government function; it only linked to hardware and houseware data.

She went out to the security barrier in the yard. I'll walk to the Ministry if I have to, she thought. Since there was no way up the wall, she climbed the oak tree. From her vantage in the boughs she saw that the area over the wall was a scoured wasteland. No grass, no structures. Nothing but burnt out, battle-scarred ground. With a hum and whir a silver gun turret atop the security barrier rotated toward her. She dropped from the tree, not waiting to find out what the automatic gun would do when it scanned her.

She paced in the yard, throwing rocks at the wall all afternoon until Simon called her in for dinner.

"I'm sorry I yelled, hon," he said. "Will you join me for some spaghetti?"

Allie loved spaghetti, and she had to eat to keep up her strength and figure out what to do.

Over dinner, she smiled back at Simon's mindless chatter about his plants and materials used to build the house. He never mentioned the world outside, and she didn't bring it up fearing he would not only yell and sulk away, but maybe fly into a dangerous rage.

After dinner, Allie told Simon she needed to be alone. He complied and gently trod upstairs to the bedroom. Allie stayed awake in the living room drinking beer. After a while, she figured Simon was asleep so she thought she'd turn the holo-screen on. She dimmed the lights. The glare disappeared from the window, revealing a silhouette of a bulky man-shape as thick as a tree. She blinked, thinking it was a trick of her eyes; then the glass shattered as the hulking green armored commando stormed in.

Allie bolted for the stairs. The giant man leapt in her way and grabbed her as she tried to squirm around him. His arms moved with a robotic whir. A cyborg. She looked up at his face. It was Big Mike, her old partner, but changed.

"Got her, boss," Big Mike said.

He dragged Allie into the kitchen as more soldiers burst in through the windows and headed upstairs. A man sat at the table flanked by soldiers bearing the indicia of the Ministry of Time and Synchronization. It was Christoffel, but he looked haggard and battle-worn. His face was tired and covered in scars. His security halo surrounded his head, shedding bristling, purple light.

"Oh Allie," he said. "If only you knew the trouble you have caused."

"It was only one wish," Allie said. "One wish, for one citizen. How much harm could that cause? I never asked for anything from the U.O.C.C. in my life."

Christoffel stood. The purple halo around him darkened.

"And the U.O.C.C. never asked anything of you," he said. "Except for you to do your job. And now, you have one more job to do. We cannot allow this wish to remain real. You must reroute it. Make it as if it never was."

"What about Simon?" Allie said.

"Do not fear for him," Christoffel said. "But he will never wish again."

"Just promise me you won't hurt him. No! Guarantee that he will finally be happy, and I'll undo it."

"All right then," Christoffel said. "You have a deal."

"Fine," Allie said, still shaken from the assault. "Then, take me to the Ministry of Wishes."

Christoffel flicked on the holo-screen. An image of the Plaza of Ministries covered in strange black metallic and fibrous webs flickered to life.

"That's not going to be so easy," he said. "The enforcers control it."

Big Mike splashed fluid on Allie's face. Pungent brine and stale sweat filled her nose and throat. Reflexively, she closed her eyes and mouth. But then she coughed and told herself she would not vomit.

"Rub it all over," Christoffel said. "In this world, the enforcers are blind but they can smell you a mile away. This will mask you."

Her body tensed as Big Mike's strong hands massaged her. After a few seconds the worst of the reek faded.

Allie, Christoffel, Big Mike, and the six Ministry of Time and Synchronization commandos loaded up onto four ATVs in the yard, three per vehicle, with Big Mike on one of his own.

As they drove, the other commandos strapped thin rectangular pads onto their armor. With their black face visors down they looked like robots. The one on Allie's ATV gave her a flak jacket and instructed her to put it on and strap the pads to it.

"What are they?" Allie asked, putting one on her arm. Her voice was tinny from her helmet speaker.

The commando touched Allie's pad. It vibrated and tickled her muscle with a small shock.

"For the webs," the commando said. "It also throws off the spiders' vibration sensors so they can't sense you move."

The ATVs passed beyond the security barrier of Simon's private town. The skyscrapers of the Plaza of Ministries loomed overhead. The once-silvery buildings were covered in black cable-like fibers. They parked the ATVs in a grove of trees on a hill overlooking the plaza. Allie didn't remember the grove being there, but this was the world warped by Simon's wish.

"It's on foot from here," Christoffel said.

"How many wasps do we have left?" Big Mike asked.

"Two tacticals and one hive," Christoffel answered. He touched a small device and two giant wasps, made of golden metal and black armor, crawled on their bellies from behind a tree. Their purplish-silver compound eyes rotated, and antennae and claws twitched, as they took to the air in a silent flutter of wings.

"Everybody ready?" Christoffel asked.

The commandos loaded what looked like blue, oversized robin eggs into squat, compact guns. Big Mike secured a few of the eggs in clasps on the metal part of his forehead. The commandos nodded.

"Okay, get that hive down here," Christoffel said. "Then launch the diversion."

Big Mike touched a device and a cloud of normal-sized wasps descended from the trees. "Stay still, Allie," he said.

The wasps swarmed around her, settling on her flak vest.

Allie watched one of the two-inch long, metallic insects crawl from her shoulder to somewhere out of her line of sight.

"W-what the hell is this," Allie said.

"You're going into the Ministry of Wishes," Christoffel said. "You'll need them. They know what to do, but only you can undo what you did, otherwise we wouldn't be here. So you just do your part and fix it, fast."

Christoffel took one more look at his team, raised his fist in the air, then lowered it. The two giant wasps took to the air and sped toward the Ministry of Dreams, far away on the other side of the sprawling plaza. The team broke from the clearing and charged for the Ministry of Wishes. Allie followed Big Mike.

Halfway down the hill an enforcer rose from its hiding place in the ground on spindly black legs that looked too thin to hold its bulky abdomen and bloated human torso. Its featureless human head turned toward them. Skin had grown over where the eyes and nose should have been. It raised itself on two legs, brandishing the sharp appendage tips.

"Fire," Christoffel commanded. "Save the muscle charges for when we get close."

Big Mike fired a round from his squat gun. A blue egg flew from it, impossibly slow. Allie thought the enforcer would skewer it with its arm or bat it away. In midair, the egg exploded with a flash of blue-white light and a flying lizard emerged, glowing blue and crackling with sparks. The little creature squawked and rammed itself into the spider-like soldier. Both the lizard and enforcer disappeared in a flash of blue light.

"What was that?" she asked Big Mike.

"Chronosaur. A baby actually. We just knocked that spider into two minutes ago, well maybe two hours from now. Plays havoc on the time-stream, but this place ain't sticking around long enough for it to matter."

"Quiet," Christoffel ordered. "Let's get down there."

The team raced to the bottom of the hill, where black cable-like webs covered the road. Allie stepped on one and her foot became stuck. The wasps covering her vest buzzed.

Christoffel scrambled to activate her shock pads. Allie's muscles jolted to life as the vibrating pads freed her foot.

"Here they come," Christoffel said.

The team activated their shockers, allowing themselves to move freely on the webs.

Dozens of enforcers crawled from the buildings and converged on the team like spiderlings hungry for a first meal. The commandos fired blue eggs and the area exploded with blue flashes and pulsing clouds of squawking chronosaurs. Big Mike grabbed Allie and charged through the strobing light toward the Ministry.

Allie saw the familiar door; plain and unadorned but for the simple government seal. It had not changed in this world, though the building was coated in black webs. Mike ripped the door open and crouched to squeeze himself inside. Allie followed.

The inside of the building looked as she remembered; an endless hallway with mazes of pipes behind the clear walls. Looking down she saw what had changed. Spider-things crowded the workroom floors. They fed black webs from their spinnerets into fittings in the pipes. The pipes pulsed, but with a sickly gray-black sheen instead of their normal orange-purple shimmer.

Allie knew it was she who had caused this and she had to make it right.

Simon's world could never last. If the Ministry of Time and Synchronization hadn't come, the spiders would have eventually infiltrated and destroyed his neighborhood paradise.

"Hold on," Big Mike said.

He smashed the walls with his giant fists. Clear fragments rained down onto the spiders working the pipes. Mike grabbed her, sent out a covering spray of blue eggs, and leapt to the workroom floor.

They landed safely in the center of the area Mike had cleared, dozens of blue-white flashes exploding around them. Enforcers emerged from the pipes forming a writhing, black circle around them.

"Get to work," Mike screamed, and fired the last of his blue eggs.

Allie touched the pipes with her hands. Without her pipe wrench the sensations and images flooded her, as they had the first day with Christoffel. Simon's wish filled the pipes. Allie focused on it. She felt sick; like she had eaten bad fish, but guided the wish through the path she had originally taken it. She pushed against the flow and circumvented filters. The current was stronger than she remembered. The pipes were choked, like clogged arteries full of images of a dark and blackened world; the wishes of the enforcers. Allie grit her teeth and pushed Simon's wish through the pipeline.

Enforcers jabbed at them from every angle. Mike beat them back with his fists, crushing their chitinous skin with each punishing blow. More and more rushed to them. Mike met one of the charging enforcers with a head butt, exploding the blue egg clamped to his forehead. He and the spidery forms near him disappeared into a blue sparking cloud. She was all alone now. The wasps on Allie's vest leapt into the air and swarmed, forming a protective cloud around her. Simon's wish was almost rerouted, only a few more sections of pipe to go. Allie felt the tips of enforcer legs pierce her. The cloud of wasps buzzed madly, a biting and stinging blur of silver. Disoriented and poisoned spiders dropped to the ground, but there were too many for just one swarm. She was almost there. More legs pierced her. She felt their poison pulsing through her just as she realized the wish had made it. She'd done it. She stared into the sightless skin-covered eyes of a charging enforcer and then the world was still.

Allie stood in at the mouth of the overflow reservoir near the new silvery pipes. Her partner, Richard, was adjusting a filter trap.

"Hey, Allie, be careful," he yelled. "You just let one get through."

Allie sensed Simon's wish in the filter trap. Richard freed it and sent it down the pipeline to oblivion.

Allie heard a click-click behind her. She turned to see two Ministry of Defense enforcers approaching, normal black robotic ones, their red-clad handlers walking right behind, not fused with them. Christoffel followed; flanked by two Ministry of Time and Synchronization soldiers.

"There she is," Christoffel yelled.

The enforcers grabbed her. She kept her hands on the pipeline but otherwise did not resist.

The robots' slender arms probed her head, capturing and removing the lizard that made up her security halo. The tiny thing gasped, impaled on the sharp leg tip. Needles pierced Allie's skin and colored flashes filled her eyes, as her memory of the world of Simon's wish faded.

"What about the husband, sir?" one of the soldiers asked.

"Take care of it," Christoffel said.

Christoffel stood over her; a sad expression overcoming his fatherly face.

"You are truly a rare talent, Allie," he said.

She was in too much pain to answer.

"In time you might have grown to be the best mechanic we ever had, so I'm sorry for this."

"Simon," she managed to say.

"I kept my word, he is somewhere safe and happy."

She felt her memories of Simon fading, traveling down a tunnel to oblivion like his wish; and then there was only the pipeline and the flow within.

RESOLUTION SEVENTEEN

Miles above the earth, steel irises opened, exposing the perfect mirrors beneath to the coldness of space. Rotors turned. Long, rectangular panels unfolded and tilted to catch the sun. Daybreak Three glimmered like a mechanical butterfly in the dark. Beams of light raced from the satellite through the unsuspecting night, creating a shining line of deadly, artificial dawn.

Far below, Xindra ran; a glowing white blur following the narrow path of light across the rubble-choked street. The eye filters in her mission suit kicked in as she glanced at her pursuers.

The Goth soldiers were engulfed in flames. One frantically unfurled its giant bat-like wings, the grafted appendages flapping in a vain attempt to take to the air. She kept running, thankful for the millimeters of reflective fiber separating her from such a death.

"Keep Daybreak Three on me," Xindra said, her suit transmitting her voice to base. "There's a lot of them."

"Only a half klick to go," Ambassador Jzent's voice answered in her ear. "Keep tight to the path and hope the weather holds." Xindra pictured Jzent at the briefing, tall and regal, her slender hands tracing the mission steps.

With the aid of her suit's eyepieces, glowing green lines appeared over the broken concrete and rebar marking the path to the bleeding facility.

"Did they see?" Xindra asked. The thought of becoming just another missing operative crossed her mind and she chased it away.

"We knew they would," the Ambassador replied. "Just a matter of what they're going to do now. Our forces massed near the border should keep attention off you."

The reflected light from above blinked out and the former industrial compound returned to the almost darkness of starlight. The ten-story tower loomed over the rest of the squat, gray, old Soviet-built buildings; pre-Ascension. A short smokestack atop it churned billowy fumes into the night.

Xindra drew a sip of blood from the tube in the corner of her lips and scanned the compound's schematic. Its main defenses were the high walls, designed to prevent a breakout, rather than a break-in.

Xindra leapt to the wall and scaled it with ease.

In the concrete yard, a dozen ragged humans roamed; pale but otherwise healthy. One lit a cigarette. Privileged ones, Xindra thought. Workers and pets. Lucky. Not like those hooked up inside.

The human with the cigarette looked up, noticed her, and ran for the door. Xindra shot him with a special bullet; a combination of sedatives and a viral agent highly contagious to humans. If I fail, at least everyone in this place will be dead or dying within twenty-four hours, she thought. A small setback in supply, but they'll feel it.

Xindra leapt from the wall to the side of the building, passing over the dazed humans below. She reached out to their feeble minds. Sleep, she commanded.

I'll need my bullets if things get tight.

The humans fell to the ground.

"Target's in a processing unit, five floors up," Jzent said.

Xindra placed a charge and blew a hole in the wall. She crawled through, concrete crumbling around her.

Debris had shattered a row of tall glass tanks. Thick, fluorescent-blue liquid puddled on the floor around them. In a wire cage in the corner, bats darted about madly; big black-eyed, red-haired, flying foxes—the fruit-eating kind. The real blood-drinking ones were tiny with nondescript wings. Constantine had told her this amusing fact long ago. She pictured him alone, out in No Man's Land, somewhere. It would be too easy to stop right now, to abandon everything to be with him again. But the world had changed with the Ascension and he did not. She forced herself to focus. Inside an intact tank a flying fox floated in fluid, its wings mutated to giant proportions. The tank cast a dim blue light on the stark concrete walls and bulky machines on metal racks.

The Soviet's biotechnology was primitive. They could only mutate and graft. Brutal. Damn Goths. They remade their bodies and dressed in the image of movie monsters from a world passed on. They had given up any link to their prior humanity with the Ascension.

"Base, reporting military activity at the facility," Xindra said. "I'm in a grafting lab."

"Copy, proceed to target."

Xindra turned the corner. The red flag of the Post Ascension Soviet Republic hung on the hallway wall. The sight of the black sickle and hammer always made her angry. Angry that the world powers now consisted of the P.A.S.R. and their opposition, an alliance of Mediterranean tribes. The rest of the globe was a devastated No Man's Land populated by scattered enclaves of humans, hungry ones, and those like Constantine who refused to or could not accept the new order.

Xindra took a sip of blood. Synthetic. Her altered organs absorbed it fast and used it efficiently. If the Mediterranean Alliance survived to see the future, maybe these advances would become commonplace, she thought.

Xindra pushed through a set of swinging double doors into a huge ward where hundreds of humans lay strapped to gurneys. The bounty of the Chechenstan raid two nights ago, she thought. Two Goth attendants pulled wires and punched buttons on an ancient machine hooked to one of the humans. Seeing her, they ran for the door. Xindra pumped them full of silver. Painful, but they'd recover, eventually.

Xindra stepped over them, noting their pasty white faces, long pointed ears (the kind recently in vogue in Prague), and oversized grafted incisors and nails. Gaudy, she thought, but nothing compared to the grotesqueries of the soldiers.

Xindra searched the gurneys and found the target. A male. Five foot ten. Late forties. She scanned his retina to be sure. It matched. She pulled him out of the restraints and slung him over her shoulder.

"Huh," the target murmured.

"Target acquired," she said.

Xindra retraced her path through the facility and jumped out of the hole in the wall. As she landed the sky filled with Goth soldiers, their bat wings spread. More and more leapt from the tower top.

"Base, wide burst on my coordinates, now!"

The first soldiers dove.

"Mission protocol says…," Jzent began.

"Mission's going to fail without it," Xindra barked, dropping to evade the first Goth. It raked her, almost pulling the target away.

Xindra rolled, holding the target close; then the world filled with light.

Her eye filters kicked in and she saw burning forms falling from the sky.

Her shoulder felt hot. Her suit had been torn. She fired her last virus bullets into the facility and ran for the secret tunnel networks leading back to Istanbul and Nevşehir.

After she cleared the wall, the artificial dawn blinked out. Narrow diversionary beams led away from the compound, lighting the dark with their false paths into the night.

Count Vladistan, the Soviet ambassador, burst into Ambassador Jzent's chambers.

"This action is a flagrant violation of Resolution Seventeen. I demand an explanation. Would you have me bring this before the Security Council?"

"My dear Count," Jzent said. "Why such an uproar?"

Xindra had returned to the subterranean city of Nevşehir from the tunnels only hours ago but had been summoned to guard Jzent. She stood in the shadows and watched.

The count squared his shoulders, smoothed his long black cape, and straightened the ruffle of his stiff white shirt.

"Solar mirrors. Satellites," he spit through his painted red lips. "You've forced us to place our ballistics on full alert."

"No need to stir up every tribe and city-state from here to Siberia," Jzent said. "What proof do you have this 'light' came from space?"

The count moved along the ancient brick floor closer to Jzent, the flames on the tall white candles flickering as he passed. Xindra watched him closely. One wrong move and I'll drag him into the sunlight myself, she thought.

"I have the coordinates," the count said. "Just admit it. I tire of these games. What did you want with Father Afendekiev anyway? We could have arranged a trade."

"We admit nothing, dear Count. And yes, we are aware you are readying your ballistics, in violation of Resolution Thirteen *and* Resolution Seventeen, I might add. They do arc into space, don't they, before landing with a big boom? I called you here to prevent a great mistake."

"You play a dangerous game with these space mirrors," said the count.

"Why, the moon is a space mirror," Jzent said matching his inflection. "Shall we issue a resolution against the moon?"

The count looked puzzled. The moon belonged to the night and could not hurt them, no matter how bright.

"To think I believed we could make progress here," the count said. "Perhaps put our differences aside long enough to invade the human holdouts in the Arctic."

"Why doesn't the great P.A.S.R. go at it alone?" Jzent said, snuffing a candle.

"With all your raids on us? And now with this new threat? We dare not."

"Or is it that the Arctic sends you enough bodies to keep your breeding lines strong in exchange for not attacking."

The count closed his cape and stepped into the shadows.

"You summoned me here to gloat, not to speak. So I leave you with a warning. Your failure to immediately disarm these threats will result in war. I have summoned the Security Council for an emergency meeting on the issue."

"Xindra, escort the count to his carriage," Jzent said, with a dismissive wave of her hand.

Xindra led the count to the stables, their footsteps echoing in the empty hallways. Just outside the count's old-fashioned, but horseless carriage, the Ambassador produced a disc from beneath his cape.

Xindra reached for it.

"First things first. You don't have to speak, just nod if you like. Jzent finally got her space mirrors off the ground."

Xindra nodded. There was no use in lying.

"What do they need Afendekiev for?"

Xindra shrugged.

"Working with them is bound for no good. Violation of Resolution One."

Xindra stared at the disc.

"See to it that there is not another space launch," said the count. "I want concrete information in your next report or I just might lose your next message."

He tapped the door under the blacked-out window and it opened with a whir. The count stepped into the plush, black interior.

"I'd reconsider my offer to join us. The coming Security Council meeting might spell the end of your precious Mediterranean Alliance."

Xindra clenched her hands. It would be too easy to rip him

apart here, leave him for the sunlight. But another just like him would take his place.

"I take it you understand. Here it is then," he said, tossing her the disc. "Tell him to spice it up. These messages have become so boring."

The door closed and the carriage rolled up the incline that led into the daylight above.

Xindra walked to her quarters though she wanted to run. Seconds after closing her curtain, she fed the disc into her player. Constantine's image appeared on the screen.

"My dear, I wish you were here," Constantine said, his slick dark hair and white face glowing in moonlight. He paced on a wooden veranda overlooking sand dunes stretching to the horizon.

"I've followed a group of wanderers across the old silk roads to this village in the Taklamakan Desert. There are no hungry ones and the fights of the city-states seldom reach here. There are enough wanderers to support us. We can live here, together, out of the way, quiet and peaceful..."

Xindra stopped the image. What would you have me do Constantine, she thought. Pretend Count Vladistan would forget where you are if I asked him nicely? Pretend there was no Ascension and disappear into the desert? It was a pretty picture, but it wouldn't last. It couldn't.

Two fighter planes painted in white-and-gray camouflage sat on the runway outside the sprawling hangar. Two human soldiers guarded each. A strange sight, Xindra thought. Metal nozzles blasted her with air as she walked through strips of plastic sheathing into the concrete-floored chamber.

Ambassador Jzent and a delegation of humans stood looking into a clean room. Xindra approached and noticed one of the olive-uniformed humans was Father Afendekiev. With his salt-and-pepper beard trimmed and hair neatly combed, he didn't look like the target she had pulled from the Goth lab. Stripes of rank adorned his sleeves. Six metal crosses, a pin of a red flaming dagger, and other medals decorated his breast pockets. The other humans were similarly dressed, shined combat boots, full uniforms, but no side arms.

Ambassador Jzent fanned her arm out gracefully to Xindra. "Sergeant Major, this is our operative who liberated you."

The delegation saluted Xindra, then made the sign of the cross in the air before their chests. Jzent and Xindra stepped back reflexively. Father Afendekiev took Xindra's hand in both of his.

"Apologies," he said. "It is our way. How can I express my gratitude?"

Xindra removed her hand.

"Your alliance with us is gratitude enough, Father," Jzent said. "Come, I want you to see this too, Xindra."

Xindra hated Jzent's show-and-tells.

Jzent ushered the delegation through plastic sheathing and into a giant bay filled with aircraft, rockets, and fuel tanks. Behind two old military-green jumbo jets, a rocket lay on a mobile launch platform the size of several tractor trailers. Xindra read the red Russian characters painted above the four flared engines, "Vlodstak." The platform's huge treads looked like they could tackle any terrain.

Xindra knew the Vlodstaks put the Daybreak satellites up, but she had never seen one this close. Before the Ascension, launches were commonplace. She had simply never cared.

Behind the rocket was another jumbo jet, a flight crew scurrying around it. Piggy-backed atop the jet rested a white-and-black craft, a shuttle with the Russian words "Buran" painted on the edge of one wing.

"It says Buran," Afendekiev said. "But it really is Pitchkita, Little Bird, the original from 1988. We recovered it in the No Man's Land."

"We've been repairing it, readying it for launch," Jzent said.

Xindra squirmed at her sing-song tone. "But, will it really fly?" she asked.

"Its sister ship has been ferrying supplies to our station at L-5 for almost two years now," Jzent said. The delegation nodded and murmured in agreement.

The L-5 station is real? Xindra thought. She'd heard about the LaGrange Point colony from other operatives, but they had all gone missing. Now, their disappearances all made sense.

"The Daybreak satellites are just a diversion," Jzent said. "Although they make quite a defense. The L-5 station is a base, an important waystation."

"To where? The moon?" Xindra said in disbelief.

"And beyond," Jzent answered.

"Side by side. Living in peace, the way it was," echoed Afendekiev.

This was much more than just violating Resolution Seventeen, Xindra thought. Jzent was showing off by spilling this information.

"We're tired of running from pole to pole every six months," Afendekiev continued. "Paying our sons and daughters in exchange for a fragile truce. Eventually the Goths won't need us anymore. We must ensure human kind has a future other than this..."

Xindra didn't see what Jzent needed the humans for. But Jzent always had a reason.

"We envy you," Afendekiev continued. "You are the ultimate space travelers. You don't need heat. You don't need air, you only need..."

"Blood," Xindra answered.

"Yes, blood," Afendekiev repeated. "But not for long. Doctor Cheslav can explain it better. He was instrumental in developing the synthetic plasma you use now."

Cheslav, the man standing next to him, cleared his throat, his jaw twitching. "We have developed a compact organ which can generate the plasma. It is transplantable."

"An artificial marrow?" Xindra asked.

Cheslav swallowed hard. Some humans had a hard time being this close to her kind.

"Like marrow, but better," he said. "Once transplanted, all it

191

needs are raw materials. Proteins and amino acids, delivered by a regular shot. Easily producible and easily transportable."

A colony in space, away from the Goths, Xindra thought. And without the need for blood. Almost like being human again.

"Xindra, we've chosen you to be one of the first few to receive the transplant and join the colony," Jzent said.

"Together, we will be pioneers," Afendekiev said proudly.

Symbiosis. Dependency. Just like the old days.

"But is there time?" Xindra asked. "Now that they know of the Daybreak satellites the Security Council will never stand for it. What if they invade?"

"They will," Jzent said. "And our best intelligence predicts they will precede any attack by firing the five to ten operational warheads they have left from the Ascension."

"Their armies will swarm over us and destroy our cities," Xindra said.

"But, we have the three Daybreak systems," Jzent countered. "And a fourth one is almost ready."

"But they know we have them. They'll just wait for a storm or cloud cover."

"We're counting on that," Father Afendekiev said. He reached into his pocket and produced a handful of tiny green pellets. He let them slip from his fingers into his other palm with a soft hiss. "Just leave that to us."

Jzent smiled and produced a disc. "False positions and decoy launch sites," she said. "Tomorrow at the Security Council meeting you will deliver this to the count."

Hulking Goth soldiers from every Soviet tribe waited outside the assembly hall of the Security Council. Sleek human-like warriors from the Mediterranean Alliance restlessly paced by the doors. Xindra watched nervously. No one had ever broken neutrality here.

With only an hour before dawn, one of the brutes approached, its oversized nails clicking on the marble. "The count is coming, follow me," he said.

She followed into the winding halls that led to the stables where the diplomats made their quick and sometimes unobserved departures. The soldier pushed open one set of stable doors, revealing the count in his immaculate black suit and velvet cape among the troughs and feed buckets.

"It's official," he said. "The Council has condemned your actions and approved the use of force. Istanbul and your dear Ambassador Jzent are running out of allies."

Xindra pulled two discs from her pocket. "Launch sites and dates," she said. "And a personal message."

The count smiled. "You made the right decision, my girl. The Motherland will remember you, maybe even grant you a position in the new territorial government."

Xindra didn't care. She only hoped that Constantine would understand why she was never coming back.

The space shuttle rested on the launch pad near the shores of the Caspian Sea, in the No Man's Land. Istanbul, Nevşehir, and Ankara had been evacuated. Dummy launch sites and decoy positions had been left behind to slow the coming swarm. The massed army dug in, in positions surrounding the launch platform.

Beneath the thick layer of pregnant clouds obscuring the sky, a boat filled with the last of the few who could not fight pushed off into the sea.

Without warning, Xindra's eye filters kicked in as the horizon burst into an orange cloud of light. Seconds later the ground rumbled. Trenches full of soldiers rattled and bounced as if a train was storming by.

Nevşehir, beautiful Nevşehir and its night-blooming gardens were gone, Xindra thought. She stared into the orange glow, imagining she could see her flat. The vine-covered cul-de-sac, with delicate white jasmine blooms and fist-sized moonflowers open to greet the night, was now just another devastated conquest of the Post Ascension Soviet Republic.

A soldier from the nearest trench flashed her a thumbs-up, then checked the watertight seals on his mission suit and motioned for her to do the same. She had, a dozen times already.

A lookout stood on a platform above the trenches, scanning

with binoculars. The orange cloud cast a surreal glow on the night. Even the moon shone red from all the burning debris

A land mine exploded, shattering the silence. The lookout shouted into his radio as another exploded, then another; each one closer. In the flashes, Xindra saw the shriveled and twisted bodies of the hungry ones. Hundreds of the insane, almost-mindless, blood-starved things (shadows of the vampires they once were) ambled toward her position. The Goths were herding them ahead of their force.

A cloud of bats swirled into the sky in a tight spiral. Xindra lifted her weapon. "Here they come," she yelled.

Behind the cover of the bats, thousands of Goth soldiers swarmed into the sky.

They are so many, Xindra thought.

With the destruction of the cities and sea behind them, there was nowhere left to retreat. No Man's Land was a battleground again.

The Goth army surged into range. Xindra unleashed a spray of bullets. Bat-winged soldiers dropped from the sky, setting off mines as they hit the ground. Mobs of hungry ones stopped to devour them, while the rest shambled forward.

The lookout dropped his radio, staring blankly at the sky as the swarm neared. Xindra fired a burst and ran for him.

"Come on!" she yelled.

He only smiled.

Xindra fired a burst at the mob then fell back toward the launch platform. Somewhere above the clouds, jet engines roared.

Tiny pellets fell from the sky, pattering softly on her suit; a rain of chemical seeds. As the whine of engines faded, the fat clouds burst, spilling their moisture onto the battle. Thousands of bat-winged forms burst into smoke as the rain pelted them. The army's anguished screams drowned any thunder. The hungry ones wriggled like insects as the cloud's water burned them, but the rain rolled harmlessly off Xindra's suit. Father Afendekiev's gambit had succeeded, she thought. His air force had blessed the clouds, then seeded them—turning the rain to holy water.

Under the cover of the downpour the humans moved out of their positions, slaughtering the retreating army. After a half hour, the clouds, empty of moisture, dissipated. A thin beam of light from one of the Daybreaks punctuated the night.

One by one, the white fighter planes, fitted with seed canisters in place of missiles, landed on a makeshift runway, a strip of packed earth near the shuttle platform.

Soldiers in full silver mission suits like Xindra's crawled from the fortifications to greet the fighter pilots climbing from their cockpits. Seeing Father Afendekiev take off his flight helmet, Xindra ran to him.

"It's a rout," Afendekiev cried. "Tell Jzent." He thrust his radio in Xindra's face. "She doesn't believe me."

"It's true," Xindra said as she surveyed the battlefield littered with corpses.

"Then we're all clear for launch," Jzent's voice answered, tinny through the speaker. "See you up there."

Human soldiers and silver-suited operatives dragged Goth corpses to a pile beneath the shuttle. Some mutated bodies still twitched. Xindra knew Constantine was not strong enough for this, or what was coming next. Though she longed to share his dream of a villa with night-blooming flowers, and a superstitious little town to prey on, she knew it would never be.

She climbed into the co-pilot seat of Father Afendekiev's fighter. The priest took them up making one final pass to ensure the airspace was clear.

The booster rockets flared to life, incinerating the bodies beneath as they lifted the shuttle into the air. Afendekiev's fighter rolled and fell into formation. Xindra sped toward the Arctic to receive her transplant, then she would journey into space in violation of Resolution Seventeen to join the ambassador in a place where it would always be night.

TEA IN THE SAHARA

"My sisters and I..."

The din of the souk filled the pause in Petra's words.

"...we have one wish before we die."

In the distance a *ghaita* sounded, the nasal reedy notes winding up a chromatic scale. Marti pictured a cobra rising from a basket.

"Don't tell him that," she said, certain the tall man had not been standing there in front of her and her sisters a second ago.

But there he was. Regarding them with his dark eyes; his skin an unreal shade of red-brown that blended perfectly with Marrakech's mud bricks. He had to be real because his smell, something masculine and exotic, cut through the aroma of sweat, cardamom, and steaming hot mint pervading the outdoor café at the edge of the bustling souk where they stood waiting for a table. The smell reminded Marti of a cologne long forgotten, perhaps one she had whiffed as a child on one of Father's guests from faraway. It conjured the earthy aromas of the Silk Road, Arabian sandalwood, and all the spices of Morocco, if such a thing could be.

Anything could be in this souk. They had purchased the green glass bottle Petra held in its crowded aisles earlier. Its long slender neck was topped with a pointed cone stopper that rose from a bulbous round base.

Despite wearing local garb, Marti thought she and Petra and Helene would be out of place, as out of place as three young women traveling alone could be. But the merchants were eager to sell and the bottle was such a whimsical and perfect thing for their wine, even if it was unlikely to withstand the rigors of travel.

Last night in celebration of their arrival, they had sat on their little balcony, smoking the last of their cigarettes, and indulged in a bottle. They toasted to the wonders of Africa yet to come. They professed their love and gratitude that they had the means and able bodies to make their journey around the globe, and that they were free of the mental bonds that kept most women back in London. The months on the road had been surprisingly good and they told each other over and over how they wished that the trip would never end. Now Petra was telling it all to this stranger; a cobra who had hypnotized both reed player and crowd.

"Don't be so uptight, Marti," Petra said.

Marti stifled her anger. Her "uptight" guidance had avoided all sorts of trouble so far, particularly a sly-tongued con man in Portugal just last week.

"I already know your wish," the man said.

And with his words Marti wasn't mad at her sister anymore. She was scared. It was something about his tone, his certainty, and the slow, calm way he spoke.

"Prove it," Petra said, twirling a strand of her auburn hair, her green eyes glinting with mischief. "Guess it and win a kiss."

"I do not want a kiss," the man said. "Three wishes is my price. But I may ask you to dance."

"Oh, la, la. Guess wrong, and *you* shall grant our every desire, *sir*," Petra said. "Expenses on you, of course. And I *may* ask you to be our guide. Deal?"

"A deal we have, young lady," he said. "You three wish that your trip will never end. You wish to live forever."

Helene gaped as if she had seen the Sphinx itself open its mouth and answer a riddle.

"I'm impressed," Petra said, taking his arm. "*Hel-lo* handsome stranger."

"Doesn't prove anything," Marti said.

But the man knew their wish. Had he been eavesdropping last night?

"Can you really grant us three wishes?" Helene asked.

Helene's childlike outbursts maddened Marti, but she knew her sister's instincts, childlike or not, were more often than not correct.

"I can give you what you desire," the man said. "But it is you three who must grant me three wishes."

"And then our trip will never end? We will live forever?" Petra said.

"Sounds horrible," Marti said, but she thought just the opposite.

"Sounds romantic," Helene said.

"Grant me three wishes and it shall be so," the man said.

She and her sisters grew up on the stories Father had read to them from picture books. Tales full of magic lamps and brave princesses outsmarting kings and handsome, long-haired efreet.

"Done," said Petra.

"Granted," said Helene.

"I'm leaving," Marti said.

In the tales, nothing was ever easy or what it seemed.

"Three sisters. Three wishes. That's how it works," the man said.

"Marti, Marti. Don't ruin this," Helene said. "At worst it will make another good story. Just say yes..."

It would make a good story, but an even better song. She could almost hear Winston, dear Winston back in London, singing in his breathy voice.

"My sisters and I...we have one wish before we die."

The footsteps and the bustle of the souk were the song's steady beat, and the murmur of bargains being struck its ethereal overture. In such a song anything was possible.

"You will see," said the man. "What I will ask of you will be easy and so very little in exchange."

Marti's instincts no longer cried danger. Her mind simply said, no way. This can't be. But beneath the logic was that part of her that so very much wanted to throw her hat in with Petra. No one's asking you to believe, it said, just to say yes. Listening to this inner voice was what had brought them out here in the first place, away from schoolbooks and potential husbands, and dreary old London.

"All right. Yes," Marti said.

The man's pursed lips released into a smile.

"My first wish is that you will do nothing to undermine our deal. Should you do so you submit to punishment as I see fit."

"Sounds austere, love," Petra said.

"Fair is fair," he said. "I could wish for a hundred things you would like much less."

"Granted," Petra said.

"Granted, easy as that?" Helene asked.

"For this wish, it is easy as that."

"Okay, then I grant it too," said Helene. "Marti?"

"Granted," Marti reluctantly said. "But I think this is stupid."

The man laughed.

"Then next you will dance for me. My second wish. Dance for my pleasure."

From the bustling aisles the miasma of voices pulsed into a driving bass, a steady heartbeat. The rhythm of the souk.

One-and-two. Three, four. One-and-two. Three, four.

In the distance the ghaita wailed. Petra grabbed Helene by the hand as if leading her to a dance floor. She giggled then threw her arms above her head and shimmied in her best impression of a belly dancer. Helene followed her lead by tracing S's in the air in front of her. She reached her hand to Marti.

"I *will* not," Marti said, and crossed her arms.

"Your beauty is such and my loneliness so profound that I would gladly waste all the world, at least waste this wish, for but just a moment such as this."

The man *was* romantic, Marti thought. And articulate in ways Winston was not. Dear old Winston who only expressed himself through his music. If he had protested or professed his love, maybe she wouldn't have left him for this journey. So, what harm could come indulging her sister's fantasy, other than some wine-induced ribbing.

She stepped next to her sisters and danced. For a moment they were his harem of three.

"There, that wasn't so hard," the man said.

"That's enough of that," Marti said and noticed that the fabric of the man's robes was moving. Changing. Before her eyes, the dusty white and tan threads unraveled and reformed into small squares of earthen brown tones, like exquisite ceramic tile. Blacks and whites, like marks on a cobra's hood, punctuated the pattern. His face too appeared composed of the same mosaic. She watched, hypnotized, willing herself to say something, but unable. Then the man spoke.

"And for the third wish—"

The entire souk became still. Merchants and buyers froze in place, currency still in hand. Patrons sat immobile at tables, holding cups of tea mid-sip. Petra and Helene screamed. Marti was afraid too, but her amazement stopped her from making any sound.

"...for the third wish, you must come with me."

The little squares composing the man dissolved into smoke. Where he had stood was now a blurred shadow in the shape of a man. Two red spheres glowed in its head where eyes should be. The air began to move. They felt themselves spinning, then the world became a whirling blur. The spinning air lifted them and in it they flew. Above the souk. Over the town. Past the red mountains and away into the Sahara.

As they crossed the sky, that exotic smell consumed Marti, making the earlier whiff seem but from an old sachet. She felt she might panic but the smell was so intoxicating, full of ginger and chocolate and musk and spice.

Before she could form another thought, the whirlwind set them down. On the sand, in the long shadow of a dune cast by the afternoon sun, tea for four had been set.

Helene staggered as if she had just disembarked a ship on wild seas. Petra yelled in exhilaration and threw a handful of sand in the air. As it fell it coalesced into thousands of little squares, all earthen colored like cobra scales. The squares spun and whirled and then only the man stood before them.

He gracefully lifted the teapot and poured. Sand streamed from it into the cups.

"I can grant your desire to live forever," he said. "But my third wish is that you must return here, to this same place every year..."

His speech lilted to the rhythm of the souk, still fresh in Marti's ears.

"...and join me for tea."

A pinprick wound opened up on Helene's finger.

"Answer with a drop of blood. The body's water of life. And drink."

Helene looked at her finger, stunned, and let the drop of blood fall into the cup. As blood touched sand the cup became filled with steaming, fragrant mint.

A pinprick opened on Petra's finger. She touched the red dot to her lips, smiled, then dipped it into the sand. It too became a cup of rich, dark mint.

When the tiny wound opened on Marti's finger she hesitated and thought of Winston at his piano.

"This trip is for us sisters, only us. You promised," said Petra, with accusing eyes.

Marti glanced at the ocean of curves and sculpted sands. Strong mint perfumed the clean, dry air. She slowly submerged her bloodied finger in the cup of sand.

The man smiled and sat, his cup now full of the same steaming mint. They sipped their tea in silence, watching the shadows of the dunes play on the sand. The evening sun sank lower in the sky.

After the sisters finished their cups, the man took one last sip and savored it.

"It is done," he said. "We return here. The same place every year. Remember."

DANIEL BRAUM

Then he too disappeared with the last dusty sunbeams stretching over the dunes. The sisters found themselves safely on the little balcony of their hotel, overlooking the souk.

Marti leaned on the rail, watching the merchants pack their wares for the night. The buyers, all the strange and wondrous people she had a traveler's kinship with earlier, now felt distant and alien as ants scurrying beneath her.

"I shall see every city," said Helene.

"And I shall seduce a man in each one," Petra said.

Somewhere far away a ghaita whined.

"Oh, what have we done?" Marti cried.

Following Petra's whimsical lead, the sisters spent months in Morocco exploring the souks and Kasbahs, losing themselves in the labyrinthine heart of Marrakech, strolling in the quiet dusty alleys of mysterious and mystical Fez, and wandering the zigzagging streets of Chefchaouen where everything was painted in dreamlike shades of light blue.

Thoughts of the strange man diminished with the new delights of each day and the sisters wondered if it had all been a dream. Besides their newfound confidence and enthusiasm, they felt the same as ever.

But all the wonders, even the mud-built cities, which looked like picture-book castles, could not keep them from their next destination. Egypt called.

Nine months after their tea in the Sahara Marti, Petra, and Helene found themselves on the Nile as guests of three gentlemen of means from Jordan. Petra had met them marveling at the Great Pyramid and they, three brothers, begged for their company.

The sisters had agreed to join them on a tour of the Nile and Valley of the Kings. One of the brothers pointed out a small, lonely shrine on the banks of the Nile near the city of Dendur, as they floated past.

"One day they will dam the Nile and the waters will rise and cover the temple," he said.

Helene found this to be the saddest thing.

When they disembarked, days later, a throng of men with camels laden with supplies were waiting for them.

Petra patted the side of one of the camels and peeked into one of the bags it carried.

"Any champagne?" she asked.

"No," one of the brothers said, with a wink and guilty smile. "It is forbidden."

"Then come up with some way to make the journey faster," she said. "Sing."

The guides started the caravan moving, a line of color and sound entering the shifting sand-brown expanse, silent, but for the wind.

The brothers sang and Marti was grateful.

That night, nestled under her shaggy brown-wool *fibule* tent, Marti heard a pop and Petra's distinct giggle. Her sister had been brought champagne after all.

The caravan set off again under the pale glow of morning, before it became too hot. As the sun rose higher the camels became unruly. A dark cloud grew in the sky just over the horizon. The men fought to keep the braying camels in formation.

"A sandstorm," one of the brothers said.

"What do we do?" Marti asked.

"It is bad," he said. "They are worried."

"We must set up shelter," said a guide.

Is there time? Marti wondered.

The cloud raced across the desert, a torrent of wind and airborne sand, bringing with it unnatural dark and a visceral howl.

Wind-whipped sand stung exposed skin as the edge of the storm reached them. The sisters covered up, but the stings were dangerously abrasive.

Their guides hunkered down in a ring, huddled against the one compliant camel. The brothers valiantly sought to shelter the sisters. Marti allowed herself to be covered.

All became dark. The wind roared but she could still hear the camels screaming and the brother above her praying. His words became screams, then moans, then all was silent.

The silence went on and on. For hours? For days? Marti alternatively shivered and sweated. She swallowed sand and thought that she would surely suffocate. Slowly she gathered her will and clawed her way out of the sand entombing her.

Half-buried in the drift was a human ribcage and beyond it a pelvis and leg bone. The guides? The brothers? All the skin had been abraded from their bones so she could not tell. Behind a great dune came a familiar sobbing. She rushed over, relieved to find her sisters, dusty and disheveled, but otherwise okay.

"He protected us," Petra said. "We cannot die."

"I thought we would be torn apart," Helene said. "Or suffocate. But we did not."

"But now we shall starve or burn," Petra said.

Marti didn't think so.

"We must trek back. East," she said. "Toward the Nile."

Marti led her sisters into the desert. Guided by the sun, they trekked east.

"I do not thirst. Do not hunger. Do not burn," Petra said.

"It is true," Helene said. "Everything he said. Everything is true."

"Keep moving," Marti said. "Or we will be lost in the desert forever."

After days under the scorching sky, they came across a caravan of British archeologists. The sisters flagged the surprised men down, and after many awkward questions and answers, passage to Cairo was arranged. The sisters recovered in the luxury of a hotel patronized by British tourists and diplomats.

"I'm going home," Marti said on the second morning of their stay. "To London. I never want to see Africa again."

"No," Petra said. "We must return. To him."

No, Marti thought. They shall have their adventures without me.

A year, to the day, after they met the strange man, Helene and Petra sat in the café outside the souk.

"Where is she?" Petra asked.

"She said she'd come. Did you believe her? It's almost evening."

The man appeared at the table. His flowing bone-white robes were free of the sand that got everywhere.

"Only you two?" he asked.

"I am here," Marti said and stepped out of the crowded souk and past the tables at the edge of the café. Winston was next to her. Sweat beaded at his forehead and neck and he looked very uncomfortable despite his linen jacket. He brandished the green, glass bottle in front of him.

Petra saw that lovesick look wash over her sister. Ordinarily it made her angry. Now it just made her hands shake.

"Sir," Winston said as if announcing a duel. "I have been told that you are powerful. But I do not believe you can get inside this bottle. I dare you to prove me wrong."

He opened the stopper.

A sour look spread on the man's face, then he laughed. As he did, Winston simply disappeared. The bottle hung in the air for a second before crashing to the ground and shattering.

"Winston!" Marti cried.

She turned around and around checking the souk for him.

"Where is he?"

"London, maybe. Or is it Shanghai or Timbuktu. I forget. Maybe he is the new man in the moon. But no matter, we are late for tea."

The sisters found themselves atop a red mountain in the Sahara. Tea for four had been set on the weathered rock. The sun hung low in a magnificent purple-red sky.

"Was our deal not fair?" the man said. "I only ask for part of one day out of three hundred and sixty-five. Three hundred and sixty-four lonely days left for me to fill."

"It was her," Petra said. "We had nothing to do with this."

"Three wishes. Three sisters," the man said. "As a consequence you will now grow old over the course of the year. Six months from now you will be middle-aged. Three hundred sixty-four days from now you will be old women. If you don't return, you shall wither into nothing. Surely this will be an adequate reminder that our deal was fair."

"It was fair. It was fair," Helene protested.

A sand-colored cobra rose from the rock. It slithered to the teacups, stopped, and showed its fangs. A bead of purple venom dropped into each cup.

"Drink," the man said.

As the sisters drank their tea the moon rose.

Was Winston really now the man in the moon? Marti wondered. Anything was possible.

The man sipped his final sip of tea and disappeared with the last of twilight's glow.

"Same time every year," said his disembodied voice.

213

As the man said, day-by-day, the sisters grew old. Six months later, they were unnaturally middle-aged. Six months after that, they returned to the souk and to the Sahara for tea which rejuvenated them. And so it was year after year. Each year they had tea in the Sahara and told the man of their lives. Helene founded a library. When she was not reading she tutored young women and encouraged them to go to university and travel overseas.

Petra took up with one playboy and tycoon after another. Her parties were known the world round, albeit under different identities in different places during different times of the year.

Marti studied the mystic arts, searching the arcane world for some clue of what had happened to Winston.

During one of their "anniversaries," just after the United States had sent a man to the moon with a rocket ship, Marti pressed the man for information about Winston.

"Where is he," she asked. "Will the Americans find him there?"

"Do you think they will be looking?" he replied. The question was as close as the man ever came to answering her.

Petra shook her head at Marti with disdain then took her cup of tea and danced in the sand. As she drained the cup Petra became young again.

When the three sisters finished their tea they found themselves on the balcony overlooking the souk. By the light of fiery braziers, the wares of the day were being put away and replaced with the oddities of the night market.

"You will help me find him," Marti said.

"I have parties to plan," Petra said.

"There is so much to read," Helene said. "I'm afraid we will see you next year."

"Same place every year," Marti said, and went into the night market seeking knowledge.

Petra traveled to California, Beverly Hills and Malibu shores, for the midsummer parties of the Hollywood elite and film business millionaires. Helene went to New York; the Metropolitan Museum was dedicating a new wing.

Marti returned to her flat in London, content to be among her crystals, alchemical powders, and books of lore. Her family and friends had all passed on, either to the grave or to lives that didn't involve their secretive, odd friend who showed up only once a year.

Then on the twenty-first of June, when due to loneliness Marti was contemplating seeking out her sisters, Winston walked through her door.

He squinted, letting his eyes adjust to the dimness and ran his hand along the hardwood banister. Marti stood at the top of the stairs looking down at him. He wore the same linen suit she had last seen him in, though it was faded and worn. His feet were bare and his beard a kinky gray mess. The weight of years showed on his skin, weathered and cracked, like the side of an old ship that had seen too much ocean. Though his eyes were bright as the full moon on a dark night. He clutched a tattered paper box under the crook of his left arm.

"Martina, is it you? Is it just another trick?" he said. "You look as young as when I saw you last."

June is a good month, wait till October, she thought, not allowing herself to feel anything. It had been so long.

"What happened?" she asked, with a rush of emotion. "Where have you been for so long?"

"I have been...," he began, then squinted and looked around again. His eyes were unfocused and Marti was certain he wasn't looking at the furniture and paintings but replaying something from somewhere far away.

"I have been walking," he finally said. "For a very long time. So long."

"From where?"

Marti didn't like the way his jaw trembled, then felt ashamed for such a thought.

"There are places you would not believe," he said.

He staggered and grasped for the banister, still clutching the box.

"I wish to tell you," he said. "And I have a gift for you. But I am so very, very tired."

Marti helped him up the stairs and into the bedroom. His skin felt coarse on her hand. His clothes musty and his breath stale.

She placed his box on the nightstand and helped him lie down above the covers. She had always thought his return would delight her, but his presence here, after all these years, felt so terribly wrong.

"The earth looks so beautiful from the moon," he said. "It was the one thing I always wished I could show you. There is no way to tell you. Only in song. But I had no instruments, only paper."

His eyes closed and Marti thought he had drifted off.

"How...," she whispered.

"There are...men...no, things that live in the moon," he whispered back without opening his eyes. "They helped me. They are cruel, but also playful. They showed me so many caves, so many tunnels, as if it were a never-ending game...and finally one day..."

Sleep took him. Marti sat there listening until his raspy breathing graduated to the grumbling half snore she remembered. In the morning, he did not wake.

Instead of weeping, as she knew she eventually would, she went to her stacks of books. Surely in them would be some way to bring him back. But he had looked so frail and worn and tired, and she stopped after only a cursory search.

She went back upstairs. The fragile old form on her bed looked at rest. At peace. She opened the box on the nightstand.

Inside were sheets of thick paper, rough and textured as if crafted by hand. She couldn't be sure but in the dim room they seemed to glow with a faint blue light. She ruffled through them. All were covered with staves and musical notes. Winston's compositions, written in indigo-black ink. They bore names like "To Marti from the Man in the Moon." All of them were for her.

She thought she would bring it to the piano in the sitting room and try to play. When she took the first sheet out, the music flooded into her. Her mind filled with the orchestrations and musings of Winston's mind, the musical residue of all his years of travel. She sat there, all day, communing with the music and the dead man's story.

Petra and Helene returned to London for Winston's last respects. The evening after the funeral, in Marti's flat, Marti told her sisters she would not be returning to the Sahara this year.

"What do you mean, not this year?" Petra said.

Marti ignored them and moved around the room. She placed a vase with fresh daisies next to a framed photo of Winston and his box of compositions.

"I mean not at all. Not ever. I'm through," she said. "Our trip is finally over."

"But you must," Petra said. "Three sisters, three wishes."

"It will be the death of us all. We shall wither and turn to dust."

"Then turn to dust we shall."

Marti stormed up the stairs.

"We must think of some way to make her come," Petra said.

She picked up Winston's photo then opened the box next to it. A blue glow leaked from within.

"It's all his fault, anyway," she said.

Petra took the box and left a note in its place.

"See you for tea," it read.

Helene and Petra sat in the sand across from Marti, a steaming pot of mint tea between them. The man stood, watching them argue.

"Where are my papers?" Marti demanded.

"Safe," Petra said. "Drink the tea. Become young again and I shall take you there."

Petra and Helene drank their tea, but remained old. Marti did not touch her cup.

Petra looked to Marti then to the man.

"Three wishes, three sisters. Tea in the Sahara. That is the way it works," he said.

"Drink," Petra cried.

"I shall not," said Marti.

"I wish you would," the man said. "My time is so lonely and you have been such a delight."

"I cannot," Marti said.

"Then so be it."

The colorful evening sky turned black. The man stepped backward, rising into the air as he did.

"No, wait," Petra said. "Surely something can be done."

The man rose over the dunes.

Helene burst into tears.

The strong steaming mint intensified. Mixed in were the aromas of sandalwood and ginger and burnt cloves and something herbal and spicy, so unique even Marti couldn't place it. It wasn't a lost smell from childhood or anything she had encountered in her wide-ranging travels. It reminded her the world was so very wide. She thought of Helene and Petra smoking cigarettes and drinking wine back that first night in Marrakech. This was the way she liked to think of them.

The man lifted higher into the sky. Helene and Petra climbed the dunes trying to follow.

"Come back, please," they cried.

The man was gone, only the moon and the first stars of night were listening.

"How will we get back?" Petra asked.

Marti thought of Winston's bright eyes. How they glowed like the moon. What strange places had he seen. She felt her skin tightening over her bones.

"Come morning, we won't survive out here very long," Helene said.

"No, we won't," Marti said.

Her sisters were all skin and bones. Skeletons draped in finery on the cool sand.

"I'm sorry, my dears," Marti said. "Our trip was so very lovely."

Before Helene or Petra could answer and before Marti could tell them she loved them, all three withered and were no more. Their dust held their shape for a second, then crumbled and blew away on the night air still perfumed with the last hints of mint.

Back at the souk, the man held a portion of fresh mint in his closed hands. He cupped them and in them appeared molten green glass, which he fashioned into a green bottle with a bulbous base.

He placed the bottle in the stall of a vendor in the night market. I hope it sells quickly, he thought and walked away, the rhythm and music of the bustling aisles enveloping him as he disappeared.

TETSUYA AND THE RANAGAREET

Lying in the dark, after bedtime, three days before his tenth birthday, Tetsuya noticed a form standing perfectly still in the corner of his room. He closed his eyes, thought of the blossoming new cherry trees it was his job to water, then opened them, but the form remained, silent and motionless. It looked like a monster.

Tetsuya sat up and thought to yell for his father, but he was almost ten and had just stopped sleeping with the nightlight on.

"You see me, Tetsuya, don't you?" asked the monster in the corner.

Tetsuya curled his feet under the covers.

"I know you're awake. Why don't you answer me?"

"I didn't think you were real until just now. And my name's Tommy."

"Tommy may be what the kids call you in school, but your given name, your Japanese name, is Tetsuya. It's important you don't forget that. And yes, I am real. Want to touch me?"

"No. I can't even see you."

The creature moved out of the corner. Not much taller than a ten-year-old boy, it shuffled past a bookshelf filled with Tetsuya's model cars and baseball cards.

"Can you see me now, or should I turn on the nightlight?"

Afraid, Tetsuya didn't answer. The monster moved, in a loping half crouch, to the bookshelf and opened the drawer where the nightlight was kept.

"Here it is," the monster said and plugged the small light into the wall.

The soft yellow glow illuminated what Tetsuya thought looked like a cross between a cat and a boy. Muscles rippled under its light brown skin. Small, bumpy ridges ran from its knees to ankles and from its elbows to wrists. Long fleshy tendrils, like thick braided hair, extended from its head and hung in a ropy mane down its neck.

"What's in here?" it said through a mouth full of thin sharp teeth, lifting the towel off Tetsuya's birdcage.

The monster stepped back and wrinkled its cat-like nose in surprise as Tetsuya's yellow canary fluttered madly in the cage.

Tetsuya's father had told him always to be brave, so he told the monster, "That's my bird Joe. Leave him alone; he just went to sleep."

The monster ran its claws across the thin bars of the cage with a rhythmic rink-tink before flopping the towel back on.

A chill ran from Tetsuya's shoulders to his groin. He wanted to cry, to yell for his father, instead he pretended he was a brave warrior.

"What's your name and what are you doing in my room?"

"My name?" the monster said thoughtfully, then paused. "I am the Ranagareet and I've come for you."

It sat on the edge of the bed. Tetsuya pulled his feet in. If it really was a monster, he would be brave, only he wasn't quite sure what to do.

"If you're some kind of a monster, how come I don't know you from my story books?"

The Ranagareet shrugged. "I'm too terrible?"

"That doesn't sound so convincing. And now you're not acting very scary."

"Don't say that. You're going to get me in trouble."

"Trouble? Are you for real?" Tetsuya asked and pulled one of its braids.

It was rough and hard; not rubber as he expected.

"Stop that! Of course I'm real," the Ranagareet said.

Tetsuya poked him. The Ranagareet poked him back.

A small dot of crimson welled up on Tetsuya's arm where the Ranagareet's thick black nail had pricked him.

"Hey! That hurt. I'm telling! Father!"

The Ranagareet leapt into the corner and disappeared into the shadows. A few seconds later, Tetsuya's father came running in.

"What's wrong?" Tetsuya's father asked, flipping on the light.

"A monster! A monster! There's a monster in my room!"

Tetsuya's father frowned at the nightlight. A hint of his colorful tattoos could be seen beneath the edge of the sleeve of his white, cotton nightshirt.

"You are a young man now, almost ten," Tetsuya's father said. "You have responsibilities. Taking care of the fish tanks and the cherry trees. Do you want me to take them away?"

"No, sir."

Tetsuya's father looked around the room, turning his head slowly and carefully.

"What did this 'monster' look like?"

"Uh, kind of like a cat, or a lizard. It sat down on the bed and then it poked me."

"Monsters do not come into young boys' rooms and sit on their beds do they?"

"No, sir."

"The light is on. See, there is nothing here."

"You're right. I'm sorry. I'll go to sleep now. Goodnight, Father."

Tetsuya's father unplugged the nightlight and placed it back in the drawer. His father turned off the light as he left. Darkness filled the room.

"See you tomorrow night," the Ranagareet said from

somewhere in the black, dispelling Tetsuya's notion that he might have dreamed it all.

Tetsuya loved the cherry trees and koi and did not want to lose his new responsibilities. He curled his feet and arms under the covers, stuck his head under the pillow, and tried to sleep.

He awoke the next day to find one of his father's plump, well-fed koi missing from the big tank in the living room, near the books and glass case with Father's swords.

"Father?" he called. But there was no answer. Today was one of the many days his father was not home for breakfast. Tetsuya did not know if he left for work early or had not yet returned from the places he went late at night. When his mother was still with them, back in Japan, she would always make him breakfast and let him sleep with the nightlight.

Tetsuya sat at the kitchen table and poured milk into his cereal. He looked out the glass doors at the line of six freshly planted cherry trees at the far end of the lush green yard. He had helped his father plant them earlier in the month; on his mother's birthday, to honor her spirit, his father had said.

Three of the slender trunks were snapped in half.

At school, he worried what his father would think. At lunch, too upset to eat, he offered his friend Emiko, the only other Japanese child in his grade, his unfinished peanut butter and jelly sandwich and packet of chocolate chip cookies.

227

"No way! Those are gross," Emiko said pushing the cookies back to him. She leaned her lanky body over the table, opened her *Princess Mononoke* lunch box, and took out a bright green box of cookies adorned with bold white Japanese writing and a smiling white anime-styled cat.

"These are *real* cookies," she said, as a spitball hit her on the ear. A group of boys at the next table laughed.

"*Bakka! Amerika-jin wa kababachi mitai futoteiru!*" Emiko yelled. The boys got up and ran into the hall.

"What did you say?"

"I said Americans are fat hippopotami."

"Aren't you an American?"

"I guess. But I'm Japanese first. Aren't you?"

Tetsuya didn't answer. He wanted to tell her about the Ranagareet but the bell rang and they rushed off to their next class.

Through the glass door leading to the yard Tetsuya could see his father in his charcoal gray suit, inspecting the fresh pale-green splinters of the snapped cherry tree trunks. Tetsuya hoped he could find a replacement before his father noticed the missing fish.

Tetsuya's father returned to the kitchen and slid the glass door to the yard closed.

"Cherry trees are auspicious to have in one's yard," he said more to himself than to Tetsuya. "It is an honor to take care of them. You are my son, and I love you. I don't understand how you could do such a thing."

"It wasn't me, sir." Tetsuya said.

He expected his father to say, "Then who was it, the monster?"

"We come from a long and proud line," his father said, unbuttoning his shirt.

Part of the red dragon on his father's chest showed. Tetsuya loved that dragon and its fiery mane.

"Some things do not change just because we no longer live in Japan. It is a very bad sign that you have done this."

"I didn't do it."

"I did not raise you to lie."

Tetsuya was not sure what his father raised him to do at all. Since moving to America, when he was seven, they went to the beach and the movies but his father never told him what he would have to do to someday wear tattoos like his.

His father pulled off his shirt, fully revealing his tattoos. The colorful ink stopped neatly at his wrists and neck. Tetsuya stared at the dragon surrounded by fire, cherry blossoms, and tiny blue Japanese characters. Bright orange-and-white koi curled around his father's arms and mingled in intricate, cerulean blue waves.

"You no longer take care of these trees. You are to go to your room and go to bed, without any supper."

Tetsuya did not know what to do or what to say. His father turned his back to him, revealing the big graceful crane on his back. Its outstretched wings seemed to gather the white-faced traditionally dressed samurai inked on his lower back. Tetsuya had recently begun wondering about the tattoos. Though his father was angry, he thought he might show him that he cared about honor and tradition, or whatever it was the tattoos meant, by asking about them.

"Father, do your tattoos mean anything?"

Interest replaced his father's stern expression. Then he carefully put his shirt back on.

"I am glad you asked this," he said. "But now is the wrong time. While you are hungry and in bed, think about what you have done."

Lying in bed, Tetsuya thought about what had happened. He thought about going to the shed in the backyard to get his baseball bat if the Ranagareet came back. He thought about his father's ceremonial swords in the glass case above the mantle in the living room.

"Two more days till your birthday," the Ranagareet said from the dark.

Tetsuya clenched his fists under the covers.

The Ranagareet stepped out of the shadows, a single pink cherry blossom tucked behind his flat, pointed ear.

"How'd you disappear so quick when my father came last night?" Tetsuya said.

"I walked through the wall."

"How'd you do that?"

"It's easy if you know how. We're mostly full of holes, me and you, and everything. So with focus and a lot of practice, even you can do it."

"I don't believe you."

"Just because you don't believe in things doesn't mean they aren't real."

"Like what?"

"I don't know, like phantoms and what I just told you."

"I don't believe in phantoms."

"My master is a phantom," the Ranagareet said.

Tetsuya noticed its forehead wrinkled with the words as if it was looking at a picture that disturbed him.

"You know what, all you've been doing is causing me trouble," he said. "If you don't leave me alone, I'll scream and my father will come again."

"If you scream again, I will kill you," the Ranagareet said.

He squinted and bore his jagged teeth in a way Tetsuya took as an attempt to appear scary.

"No, you won't," Tetsuya said.

The Ranagareet raised his arms and extended his clawed fingers. Tetsuya didn't like those claws.

"If you try to take me away, I'm going to fight," Tetsuya said.

The Ranagareet stopped making his scary face. He appeared confused, then, after a second, disappointed.

"I don't want to fight," he said. "My master told me to say

those things if you gave me any trouble."

Tetsuya unclenched his fists.

"But really, I have come to take you away, on your tenth birthday. I'm supposed to torture you until then."

"That's not fair! What did I do?"

"It's not that you did anything. But you're your father's first boy and soon you turn ten."

"I come from a long and proud line," Tetsuya said, repeating his father's words not knowing exactly what they meant.

The Ranagareet ran to the bed.

"No matter what he thinks, your father is a failure. He is a criminal who fights with guns. That is why you are here in America."

Tetsuya clenched his fists again.

"Don't you dare say my father has no honor."

"What do you know of honor?" the Ranagareet said.

"Did your master tell you to say that too? What do *you* know of honor? Is it honorable for you to bother me like this? I'm just a boy."

The Ranagareet hunched his shoulders and chewed on one of his nail tips.

Tetsuya got out of bed and stood as straight and tall as he could.

"You act like you don't even want to be here. So let's get on with it, or get out of my room. I have a baseball game tomorrow and I want to get to sleep."

The Ranagareet continued chewing and glanced at Tetsuya out of the corners of his eyes.

"Baseball?" he asked.

"Yeah," Tetsuya said.

The Ranagareet walked to the bookshelf.

"That sounds like fun," the Ranagareet said, picking up a model car.

"It is."

They stared at each other for a few long seconds.

"Come on," Tetsuya said. "Will you please just go away?"

"It's not up to me. Hey, can I have this car?"

"You want my car?"

"Yeah."

"Okay, it's yours," Tetsuya said. "But only if you go."

"And this one?" the Ranagareet said, picking up another car.

"Sure," Tetsuya said.

"And this one?" the Ranagareet said holding all three in the crook of his arm.

Tetsuya sighed.

"Come on, not that one, put it back."

The Ranagareet looked up and down the bookshelf but held on to the car.

"Okay. Take it. But then do we have a deal and you'll leave me alone?"

"My master, Lord Ginsho, said 'no deals.' But I'll leave you for tonight."

He spun the wheels of one of the cars as he walked into the shadows.

Tetsuya thought to look up the name, Lord Ginsho, in his father's books.

"Oh, by the way, can I have some chocolate cake?" the Ranagareet asked from the dark.

"No. And don't take any. You're going to get me in more trouble."

"Goodnight. See you tomorrow," the Ranagareet said, and made a sound like a speeding car.

"No toys! Smash them! Smash all of his toys! Kill all of the fish! Knock down every tree!" said a voice in a dusty, dark basement of the Metropolitan Museum of Art.

Crates rumbled and clanked, sending up small clouds of dust and knocking the Ranagareet off the box marked Asian Gallery which he had been sitting on.

"But, Lord Ginsho, I took the best fish and ruined the three nicest trees," he said to an empty suit of black samurai armor inside a pried-open wooden crate.

The Ranagareet looked at the elegant curve of the long, sharp crescent adorning the angled steel helmet. No eyes were present under the helmet, but he felt Lord Ginsho's presence.

"It's not enough," Lord Ginsho's disembodied voice said.

The Ranagareet dropped to his knees before the crate.

"Please, Lord Ginsho," the Ranagareet said. "Don't send me back to do more."

"Do not beg! Begging is dishonorable. I thought I taught you not to beg."

"Yes, Master," the Ranagareet said, and he remembered.

When he was still a boy in Japan, days before his tenth birthday, the Ranagareet awoke in his bed to the feel of small, strong hands on his neck.

A cat-like face pressed up against his. Cold, hard eyes looked directly into his. "You are coming with me," it snarled.

"Please don't kill me," the boy who would become the Ranagareet pleaded.

He never celebrated his tenth birthday. The creature carried him away to a museum and placed him in a gallery of suits of samurai armor. One suit of armor rattled and a dry whisper filled his ears, though he saw no one.

"Your family is without honor and you must pay the price," the voice the Ranagareet came to know as Lord Ginsho's said.

"Anything, please don't kill me," he said.

"Do not beg. This is your first lesson," Lord Ginsho said.

Ginsho's phantom form materialized in the armor; a short, solid ox of a man with raven-black hair and a long moustache that hung down below his chin. His eyes empty, black voids in the places where eyes should be.

The cat-like creature bowed to Lord Ginsho's phantom.

"I have brought you the boy," it said. "Will you release me now?"

Dozens of suits of armor rattled on their stands, straining to break free.

"In the morning," Lord Ginsho said. "You will be free in the morning."

Lord Ginsho turned to the boy who would become the Ranagareet.

"Your training begins immediately. You must learn to focus, this way you can see me even when I am not expending energy. Sit on the floor. Cross your legs. Place your fingers together. Form a triangle. Concentrate on your fingertips. Feel the ki running through them."

"I don't feel anything."

"Sit there, until you can feel it. You'll know. Your fingers will tingle like never before."

Over time he learned how to focus, how to see and speak with spirits, and even how to walk through walls and become invisible. His body began to harden and change into the form he walked in now. After that first night he never saw the creature again.

"I'm sorry, Master, I remember. I will not beg," the Ranagareet said.

The black armor creaked and groaned as if an unseen force were trying to jam it together. The Ranagareet hated the sound.

"The world is full of those who do not honor their ancestry, and

I am but one warrior," Lord Ginsho said.

"You have me, Master."

"You are a failure."

The black gauntlets in the open crate creaked and shook as they slowly turned. The Ranagareet swallowed and ran his hand over his neck.

"You are strong, Master. Why don't you gather the boy yourself?"

The gauntlets shook faster.

"I made you so I would not have to waste my life force on such tasks. But you cause more trouble than you are worth."

The Ranagareet tried to focus so he could be ready to escape if Lord Ginsho attacked him. It took him longer to focus when scared.

"Smash the toys!" Lord Ginsho yelled. "Now."

Ginsho's armor settled back into its crate. The Ranagareet swallowed in relief.

"Bring me Tetsuya Kimura tomorrow. Then our time together will be finished," said Lord Ginsho's voice.

"Where will I go?" the Ranagareet asked. "Will I have toys and be able to eat cake?"

Lord Ginsho did not answer.

"Lord Ginsho?" the Ranagareet asked the empty suit of armor.

After a minute with no reply the Ranagareet picked up one of his toy cars and ran it along a wooden crate, before smashing it to pieces as instructed. After he delivered Tetsuya to Lord Ginsho, he hoped he would wake up as a boy again.

The Ranagareet focused as Lord Ginsho had taught him. The solid objects around him became soft and blurry. He sensed every molecule in his body and the spaces between them. Once he felt the spaces between the molecules of the wall match the locations of his molecules, he passed through the museum's thick, stone walls and headed to Tetsuya's house for a piece of chocolate cake.

Emiko punched the floppy baseball mitt that hung on her hand. Barrettes adorned with smiley-faces held her jet-black hair in pigtails.

"I love baseball. I wish they didn't always stick us way out here."

Tetsuya watched the shortstop scoop up a ball and throw it to the second baseman.

"Hey," Tetsuya said. "Does your dad have tattoos?"

The next batter walked to the plate.

"No, stupid! Only the lower class and criminals have tattoos." She laughed. "What do you think my father is? Yakuza or something?"

"What's yakuza?"

"Yakuza. They're like the mob. Only Japanese, not like those guys on T.V. from New Jersey. That's such a silly question. What's wrong with you?"

"Let me ask you something," Tetsuya said. "If there was a monster that kept coming to your room, what would you do?"

"You really are weird." She laughed again. "Monsters aren't real."

"If they were real, what would you do to make it leave?"

"That's easy. Find out what it wanted and give it to it."

"But what if you already tried that. What if it only wanted to take you away?"

"That's easy, too. You'd have to fight it."

The batter hit the ball. It sailed into the far outfield and rolled into the trees behind them.

"Whee! Finally getting some action out here! Let's go, Tommy!" she said mockingly, and followed the ball into the trees.

Tetsuya ran in after her. After a second he didn't hear the crunch of her footsteps.

"Emiko? Did you find the ball?! Where are you?"

There was no answer. A gray squirrel stood on its hind legs, still and alert. Tetsuya's shoulders tingled.

"I have her," the Ranagareet said calmly, from somewhere in the trees.

Tetsuya scanned the low branches. Nothing. Not even a falling leaf or a moving shadow in the afternoon sun.

Tetsuya realized the Ranagareet would not just bother him in his bedroom. It had his only friend and had ruined his game. And it was coming to take him away tomorrow.

"Come out and show yourself," he yelled.

"Sorry. I'm bringing her to show my master how much I've been torturing you. After I deliver you, he's going to take me home."

"Emiko!" Tetsuya yelled and ran deeper into the trees.

"Catch," the Ranagareet whispered, from somewhere above.

The baseball sailed out of the trees and clocked Tetsuya in the head.

Tetsuya sat next to his father, across from the principal's big desk. His head hurt.

"This is very serious, and very strange," the principal said. "Girls just don't disappear. Your son says a monster took her."

Tetsuya flinched. He was in big trouble now.

The principal looked at the police cars outside the window, then held up a crude drawing of the Ranagareet Tetsuya had made.

Tetsuya's father took the picture, glanced at it briefly, and then shook his head slowly, almost in sync with the principal.

"I'm sorry, sir," Tetsuya's father said. "He was hit in the head."

"Yes, we're glad he's all right, but I wanted to talk with you myself, before you see it on the evening news or something."

"Thank you, sir."

His father was silent the entire ride home. They pulled into the driveway. Tetsuya saw the rest of the cherry trees had been broken. He saw the puzzled look on his father's face as he noticed too.

"I'm punished again, aren't I?"

Tetsuya's father took out the picture of the Ranagareet.

"You're not punished," he said. "Get some rest. If you cannot rest, think of what you would do to fight this monster."

He believes me, Tetsuya thought. He smiled and it made his forehead hurt.

"I'm going to see Dr. Keiju," his father said. "Stay inside until I return."

Tetsuya ran to the house as his father backed out of the driveway and sped away.

Tetsuya did not want to rest. He crossed the living room and stopped at the glass case above the mantle with the swords and knives. After a moment of staring, he opened the case and removed a small, thin sword. He could see his reflection in the blade. He swung it. The small Japanese characters etched near the edge blurred as it cut the air with a satisfying hiss.

He put the sword back, leaving handprints on the glass as he closed the case. Then he pulled a chair to the bookshelf next to the mantle and took down a few of the old books from the top.

The first book he flipped through contained hundreds of portraits of samurai annotated in Japanese writing. Were these family members, Tetsuya wondered? He couldn't read the writing well but his father always reminded him he came from a long proud line. Tetsuya pulled a newer looking book from the bottom of the shelf. It was filled with old black-and-white photos. He stopped on a page with a posed shot of a group of tattooed men wearing loin cloths outside a ritual bath. Each man's tattoos stopped neatly at their neck and wrists. Tetsuya squinted and all the inked designs blurred into one image.

The front door opened and Tetsuya's father walked in, holding a paper bag. He looked at Tetsuya and the open books. He placed the bag on the table and took out smaller bags of herbs, incense, brightly colored paper, and a length of silver rope.

"What's all that, Father?" Tetsuya asked.

His father wiped the hand print from the sword case and smiled. He opened the glass door by slipping a finger into a groove along the top and popping it open.

"See, this is how you open it without leaving a mark," he said to Tetsuya and took out a knife. He placed it on the table next to the open book and looked at the photograph.

"Is it true only criminals have tattoos?" Tetsuya asked.

His father looked at him and then at the photograph.

"One person's criminal is another's hero," he said.

"What about you? Have you done something to lose your honor? Is that really why we moved here?"

"Who told you that?"

"The creature. He says that's what his master, Lord Ginsho, told him. Is he a criminal too?"

In response Tetsuya's father stood on the chair, pulled down a few books, and flipped through them.

"Lord Ginsho is one of our ancestors. Here," he said, showing Tetsuya a portrait of a short, stout man in regal black armor. An elegant black crescent adorned the helmet the man held at his side.

"Lord Ginsho once led an imperial force to hunt down rogue samurai who had abandoned their honor. Ginsho conscripted their sons into his service but the Emperor had him killed because Ginsho began deciding himself who had lost their honor."

"Lord Ginsho is coming for me?" Tetsuya asked.

"Not many remember him and those that do, do not pay him respect. Thus he is weak and his power wanes. That is why he sends the creature."

Tetsuya's father handed him the knife.

"It will come again tonight and you will fight it."

Tetsuya pictured himself in the dark without the nightlight holding the knife under the covers. He wanted to say he was afraid.

"I will be waiting in the closet," his father said. "Everything will be fine and we will rescue your friend. Go get ready for bed and I will be up soon."

"I am worried about Emiko," Tetsuya said at the top of the stairs. "But I'm not afraid," he added, even though it was not true, because that was what he thought his father wanted to hear.

Tetsuya clutched the knife as the Ranagareet stepped out of the shadows.

Joe the canary fluttered madly in his cage.

"I have to take you now," the Ranagareet said. Tetsuya detected sadness, but also a new resolve in his voice.

The Ranagareet held up his claws and made a scary face. "Come on. Let's make this easy."

"If you go away I'll give you all my cars!"

The Ranagareet's nose twitched, but he kept his scary face and he moved closer.

"If you take one more step, I'm going to fight you."

The Ranagareet stopped. Tetsuya thought he was struggling not to cry.

"I'm sorry. But I'm really sick of being like this," the Ranagareet said and held up his claws.

They looked at each other silently. Tetsuya opened his mouth to speak but the Ranagareet pounced. Tetsuya screamed and stabbed with the knife. The metal slid off Ranagareet's hard skin.

Tetsuya heard his father burst from the closet. The Ranagareet quickly took control and sat on top of Tetsuya, pinning him. One clawed hand covered Tetsuya's mouth and the other held both Tetsuya's hands over his head. Tetsuya squirmed while the Ranagareet closed his eyes and tried to focus. Then the world became soft and blurry. Tetsuya saw his father moving toward him, a length of silver cord in his hand like a lasso, before he and the Ranagareet disappeared.

Tetsuya found himself in a dark basement. The Ranagareet held him at the foot of a crate full of old black armor.

He scanned the room and saw Emiko's mitt on the floor, then

he saw her lying motionless in the corner, leaves from the field still stuck in her pink high-topped sneaker.

"Emiko," he yelled.

She didn't answer.

The armor in the crate before him creaked and rose into the air. Lord Ginsho appeared, filling the empty spaces between the floating pieces of armor.

"I'm not afraid of ghosts," Tetsuya said, though he wanted to break free and run.

"That is a good start," Lord Ginsho said. "I hope you are a fast learner."

"Master. Now will you release me?" the Ranagareet asked.

"One more task. Return to his house and destroy it."

The Ranagareet bowed and dematerialized. Tetsuya ran to Emiko. Cuts and claw marks covered her, but her chest still rose and fell. Tetsuya screamed and ran around the room pushing over crates and swords.

"Good. You're a fighter," Lord Ginsho whispered, his voice cold as the threat of snow in spring.

The Ranagareet materialized outside Tetsuya's house, a can of gas and matches in his hand. A silver Lexus idled in the driveway. The Ranagareet passed through the wall into the kitchen and grabbed a cookie. He figured he'd take another of Tetsuya's cars before starting a fire.

As he stepped into Tetsuya's room he felt his arms pull against his sides. He looked down to see a thin, silver rope wrapped around him. The rope tightened and he was yanked into the room and slammed into a wall.

"In here. I have him," Tetsuya's father called. "Bring my sword!"

The Ranagareet struggled to free himself from the silver cord. Tetsuya's father pulled it tighter. Two young Japanese men in suits ran into the room and grabbed him.

Tetsuya's father stuffed herbs in his mouth and bound the rope around the Ranagareet's arms and ankles. He tied the remaining rope around his neck like a leash. The Ranagareet tried to dematerialize and escape but found he could not. The silver rope burned where it touched him.

They led him outside to the silver Lexus in the driveway. One of the young men sat behind the wheel. The other stuffed him in the back seat between himself and Tetsuya's father.

"Take me to my son," Tetsuya's father said.

The Lexus pulled up outside the Metropolitan Museum of Art.

"Turn invisible," Tetsuya's father ordered.

"It hurts," the Ranagareet said, rolling his neck.

The young man holding the leash tugged on the silver cord to check it. The Ranagareet and the cord binding him disappeared.

Tetsuya's father placed his sheathed sword down his back beneath his jacket. He, the young man, and the Ranagareet exited the car and walked up the long, wide stone stairs into the museum.

"Two," said the man holding the Ranagareet's leash to the woman in the ticket booth.

"The museum will be closing in twenty minutes, sir, tomorrow's hours are..."

"That's fine," he said and paid her.

They turned right, walked through the crowded lobby, and stopped at the service elevator near the Egyptian gallery. After a moment, the doors slid open.

"Sorry, this elevator is for museum personnel only," the guard inside said.

Tetsuya's father struck the guard's neck with the heel of his right hand. The Ranagareet noticed the quickness and straightness of the strike. The guard gasped for air and fell. Tetsuya's father caught him. The young man led the Ranagareet into the elevator. The doors closed.

"Show yourself," Tetsuya's father ordered.

The Ranagareet wanted to refuse but found he could not. He made himself visible. The silver cord hurt and he felt groggy from the herbs.

"Which floor?" Tetsuya's father asked.

His man bound and gagged the guard.

"Down. All the way down," the Ranagareet said.

The elevator descended. Tetsuya's father took off his jacket and unsheathed his sword.

The elevator doors opened into a vast dimly lit basement,

crowded with labeled boxes and long wooden crates.

"Where is he?" Tetsuya's father asked.

"The door at the end," the Ranagareet said.

"Stay here," Tetsuya's father said to the young man. "Any problems, kill it."

Tetsuya punched Lord Ginsho, bloodying his knuckles on the hard armor. Lord Ginsho held him back with one black gauntlet planted squarely on his forehead. Tetsuya yelled and screamed and swung his fists.

The boom of a door crashing open rang out from somewhere behind him. The sound of sure quick steps on the stone floor rang through the room. Then Tetsuya saw, in a blur, his father planting a solid side kick into Lord Ginsho.

Lord Ginsho released him and he fell forward. He crawled toward the corner where Emiko lay. One of the swords on the floor rattled and shook as he passed it. The sword rose into the air, flew to Lord Ginsho, and hovered before him. His father faced the phantom in the rattling suit of black armor and gracefully traced a circle in front of him with his sword.

"Criminal," Lord Ginsho whispered.

"Traitor," Tetsuya's father replied.

Tetsuya's father charged, thrusting with quick, tight jabs. Lord Ginsho's sword spun and parried, blocking each attack.

They moved as if dancing. Silently. With only the groan of Ginsho's armor and the clank of metal on metal from each sword strike.

Tetsuya's father pushed forward with a series of quick thrusts. He stepped inside the sweeping arc of Lord Ginsho's block and struck Ginsho's helmet with the palm of his hand. As the strike connected, Tetsuya's father released a deep, resonant yell. Tetsuya felt the sound in his chest. Ginsho's helmet flew into the air and landed on the stone floor with a rattle.

Tetsuya released Ginsho's head, and all his unarmored places had become even more transparent. He could see right through them to dark walls behind him. Ginsho's sword was unaffected. It twirled in a mad spiral, forcing Tetsuya's father back, blocking as fast as he could.

With each strike of Tetsuya's father's sword a piece of Ginsho's armor fell to the basement floor and Ginsho's form became more and more transparent. After dozens of hits, Lord Ginsho was almost too insubstantial to see. Ginsho brought his sword back to strike at Tetsuya's father's head. Tetsuya's father stepped in with a fast side kick, connecting with Lord Ginsho's chest plate. All the remaining pieces of black armor fell to the ground and rattled like a broken skeleton.

"Criminal!" Lord Ginsho's disembodied voice whispered.

Tetsuya's father stomped on the pieces of armor. They shattered like brittle bones beneath his boots.

"You destroyed him," Tetsuya yelled.

Tetsuya's father ran to him, picked up Emiko, and placed her over his shoulder. Then he pushed Tetsuya through the room and toward the door and the elevator.

The young man holding the Ranagareet's leash waited for them.

"One more thing," Tetsuya's father said.

He handed Tetsuya his sword, then pulled the Ranagareet out of the elevator. He pushed him to the floor and placed his foot on the creature's back just below his neck.

Tetsuya's father stood behind Tetsuya, placed his hands over his, and helped him lift the sword.

"Bring it down on his neck in one smooth stroke," he said.

"Don't do this," the Ranagareet said. "Please just take me home."

Tetsuya paused and looked up in his father's eyes. He didn't want to kill the Ranagareet, but knew he would never have his father's respect if he didn't act decisively.

Tetsuya brought the blade down. He felt the power of his father behind him, guiding him, giving him strength. The sword hissed, cleanly cutting through the Ranagareet's neck. Instead of blood, sparks and a luminous white fluid sprayed out. The Ranagareet's body twitched and began to dematerialize. For a second a young boy lay on the floor surrounded by fluid and fading sparks, then all trace of the Ranagareet was gone.

Tetsuya and his father got out of the silver Lexus and stepped into the New York City street.

They walked through an unmarked, gray steel door into a huge, dimly lit parlor crowded with tables full of Japanese men. Smoke and the crack of playing cards slapping down on tables filled the air. Elegant screens decorated with black Japanese ink paintings separated some of the tables far in the rear. Tetsuya's father led him to one of the back tables and motioned for him to sit down, across from an ancient Japanese man in a loose-fitting black suit.

Tetsuya's father bowed. Tetsuya did the same.

"Dr. Keiju, this is my son, Tetsuya," Tetsuya's father said proudly.

Dr. Keiju scratched the white stubble on his chin and peered at him with dark green eyes.

"He is very young to have killed."

Tetsuya's father took the drawing of the Ranagareet out of his pocket and placed it on the table.

Dr. Keiju looked at the paper, then at Tetsuya.

"Is this true?" he asked.

"Yes, sir," Tetsuya answered.

Dr. Keiju nodded. "Take him back then."

Tetsuya followed his father and the old man to an unremarkable door on the back wall of the parlor. The small room beyond the door was brightly lit. The big chair in its center with the rack of tools next to it reminded Tetsuya of a dentist's office. Tetsuya sat on the big chair and Dr. Keiju slipped a fat telephone book underneath him.

"Take off your shirt," Dr. Keiju said.

Tetsuya complied. Dr. Keiju removed the paper covering from a needle on the tray of tools, then picked up a felt-tipped pen. He drew a single Japanese character on Tetsuya's arm, then the outline of what looked like the Ranagareet's face on his chest.

Tetsuya's father opened a cabinet, took out an unmarked bottle of clear liquid, and poured a shot for Tetsuya into a small ceramic cup.

"Drink," he said.

Tetsuya drank a sip and spat out the rest. He felt his insides warm as the needle neared his skin.

"I am proud of you, son. We will plant new trees, and shop for new fish. It will be your job to take care of them."

Tetsuya flinched as the needle pierced him. His father smiled as the first drops of ink entered Tetsuya's skin.

"Happy birthday, son," he said. "Tomorrow we will begin your training."

THE TRUTH ABOUT PLANET X

Planet X is racing toward Earth. It's somewhere out there beyond the Kupier Belt right now but before long it's going to crash down in the center of the Las Vegas strip. No one else knows. Well, I've told my publisher, shouldn't have done that, but she doesn't believe me. I've told my bearded dragon, Larry, too but he's been sleeping for months and it's long past time for him to wake up.

I place my ink cartridges and fresh needles gently atop my old suit that Sarah folded and placed into my luggage. I glance over at Larry's tank hoping to find his sentient, knowing gaze looking back at me. His beige-scaled eye coverings are closed. Rows and rows of spiky triangles every color of the sand cover his plump body. His tail and limp limbs have shifted position since last night but he's still hibernating. Still half in the darkness of the hiding spot under his basking place.

Sarah brings me the rest of my tattoo gear and I place it in the luggage.

"Anything else?" she asks.

She's grown into her wiry athletic frame and blossomed into a woman. A woman I barely recognize. No longer the little girl I helped tumble and flip in our father-daughter at-home gymnastics routine I used to love to show off.

"Spray Larry down," I say. "Once a day. Hornworms and fresh greens are in the fridge in case he wakes up when I'm gone."

"I know what to do, Dad."

I worry she'll forget. Or decide not to. She's no longer fascinated by the green, wriggling caterpillars Larry loves to chomp but she's a good girl. And comes by to see me even when she's not helping out. But Larry is just a lizard and needs someone.

"Maybe I shouldn't go," I say. "I want to be here when he wakes up from hibernating."

"Bruminating. Not hibernating. It's different, Dad. Bruminating looks a lot like hibernating but it's not. There's no loss of weight. He lowers his metabolism so he can get by on low levels of water and oxygen."

"It's already spring. He never stays asleep this long."

"It has nothing to do with *our* weather. Or our years or seasons or anything. I think it relates to the dry and wet cycles of ancient Australia. That's where lizards like Larry are from, Dad, and they were so, so old even when humans were young."

"You know a lot about Larry."

"You always made me read."

"Don't you think he's sad you don't want him anymore?"

"Dad. You've had him for how many years?"

"Seven."

"I think he's happy he gets his nice big tank that would never fit in my dorm. And he's happy I'm looking after him."

"You think so?"

"No. I think he doesn't notice."

"I'm not going."

"Dad. You worked hard on this show. You already paid to have your canvases flown out. Extra leg room for some of them. Plus *she's* gonna love it. She's going to green light the book the way you want it. And Larry will be fine."

"I'm not worried about Larry."

"I'll be fine, Dad."

"You don't want to see her?"

"No. I mean...I have school."

"I'm not worried about you or her."

"Then what's up, Dad?"

"Nothing."

She brings me the rest of my tattoo gear and I place it in the luggage. She's almost twenty-two. I still see her as the old "her" sometimes. The *her* that lifted off her body and left it behind and went up through the sky, into space and to Planet X. Now that

Planet X is coming I wonder what's going to happen to those who survive.

Planet X is the place where all of our old selves go. Our selves made up of the feelings, dreams, and the compassionate wide-eyed selves we used to be and shook off somehow as part of growing up. Or just growing out. These selves go somewhere. In preparing for this show I finally realized they go to Planet X.

Sarah is smart. And she always believes me. She worries. She knows something is wrong. I can't keep this from her.

"Honey bunch? Let me ask you something. Would you believe your pop if I told you there is a place where all our lost selves go?"

She takes the boarding pass she has printed for me from the printer, places it on my luggage so I won't forget, cocks her head and looks at me. I see traces of the contour of her little girl face that looked at me the same way when I first told her Mom wasn't coming home anymore. Her Mom is an artist.

"What do you mean lost selves?" she asks.

"Our selves who used to be. You know, like the "you" who loved Larry. The "me" who wasn't a tattoo artist."

We both know this means the "me" before her mom left.

"I see where this is going. I don't want to go and see Mom. Plus I can't. I have exams."

"I didn't mean that."

"Okay. Okay. Even if I believed you. Why a place?"

"A place. Like a planet. Maybe there is a planet where all these old selves go. Maybe now in these crazy times it's coming back.

Coming back to Earth to bring everyone back. Bring us back to ourselves and make everything all right."

"But still. Why a planet? Why would they need a planet? Why not a spaceship or a giant turtle or something?"

"I don't know. I don't know that they need a planet. I just know it is a planet."

"You know?"

"I know. I just do."

"Okay. Going with you for a second. But I'm thinking how do you know this *planet* isn't full of demons, or aliens, or alien-demons hitching a ride?"

"What? Why would you say that?"

Because she's my daughter, that's why.

"I don't know. If I were a demon it's what I'd want to do to thwart that squishy feel-good coming-home plan. I don't know how exactly I would but it's how I'd try to wrench things up."

The notion is too disturbing to comprehend or even think about anymore. We're done talking about Planet X. But it doesn't matter. We're almost out of time and the car is here to take me to the airport.

I feel them on Planet X. The people who are no more. The castoffs. The shadows of the selves left behind here on Earth. I see them. Not sure if it's in my mind's eye, or what, but I see them. Lifting their arms. Stretching them wide. Sarah is among them. The

Sarah who used to be. The Sarah who wanted to be taken to the pet store to see the cute boy who worked there. The Sarah who demanded we come home with Larry. She used to carry him around, his little hatchling lizard-self clutching to the front of her shoulder. She used to hand feed him greens and delight in the way he chewed. I always knew "this Sarah" was still out there, somewhere. Now on the eve of my trip to Las Vegas I know that place is Planet X. Planet X, Sarah, and all the people on Planet X are made of the cast-off hopes and dreams of the people of planet Earth. They're not demons. No matter what my darling daughter says.

In Las Vegas I am a man of stone walking through the casino floor. My arms. My legs. My skin. My hands. My heart. All stone. All heavy. The only thing allowing me to move is the lightness of the artist and the young boy I'm walking with.

I'm living out my *Fear and Loathing in Las Vegas* dream with them.

The "artist," as everyone calls her, is my publisher. And Sarah's mother. We used to be married. People started calling her the artist when we got divorced. Some sort of a name thing. A Prince thing? I don't know. Now she insists on it.

A few minutes ago at my room party she was coming on to the boy way strong. She pulled out a joint and they were going to step outside to smoke when I said, "Stop I'm that young man's attorney."

"Really," she said. "I can't tell when you're serious anymore. Are you an attorney now too, Jaya?"

"Yes, I'm serious. As his attorney I command you to smoke that joint."

"He's not serious. Let's go smoke," she said.

"She's right. I'm not an attorney. I just love that movie and always wanted to say that. Especially now since Planet X is coming."

"What? Did you say Planet X?"

"You know it?"

"You mean that thing they call Niburu," the boy said. "Are you an astronomer or something?"

"I'm just a tattoo artist and she's my publisher and we're here for World Ink."

"We're going to get a burger at Johnny Rockets after we smoke this, Jaya," the artist says. "I guess you could come."

The boy walks through the casino floor with us but he is not made of stone. The artist is not made of stone either. She is made of chromium steel. Plated rebar and platinum on top of that.

The "boy" is a young tattoo artist not much older than Sarah. His hands are slack and at his sides, but they might as well be outstretched, like in that movie with Bruce Willis, where at the end he is taking in all the feelings of all the people in the train station. I can tell the boy is feeling all the hopes, all the dreams, whatever passions are left of these masses sitting blindly in front of the slots.

Hundreds of the brightly lit machines form rows and rows and rows. Neon pinks and blues and greens. Photorealistic art advertising fantasies of every flavor. Sherlock Holmes. Ancient Egypt. Sexy Showgirls. Firing noise and light at us. Tempting us with their digital opium.

The boy doesn't have an empathy shield. Not yet. Well I guess he won't ever 'cause it's too late. It is almost the end. Before I met Sarah's mother I wasn't made of stone. I didn't have a shield. It was part of what I thought she loved about me.

A young couple not much older than the boy, or Sarah, drag an exhausted toddler past us and plop down on the seats in front of slot machines with Egyptian sphinxes on them. It's two a.m. The three of us watch silently as the young girl fights to stay awake. She fights to make sense of it all. She doesn't dare care. Her face tells us she's too afraid.

Then what looks like an exact copy of her, right down to her pink sweat suit and all, peels off and separates from her little body. Her old self. This detached self, floats up and disappears through the casino ceiling. She's going to Planet X. The boy can't take it. He's overwhelmed by the tragedy of it all and can't stop his tears.

The artist comforts him. Sometimes I think she's a bitch. A diva. Even a predator. But she is showing compassion. Her shield is down, just enough to let him in. I would have never have guessed it but somehow she has made a true connection with him.

"Even in Las Vegas there is hope," the artist says to him. "Even here."

I didn't think she had it in her. At least not anymore. I knew she once did.

"Even though Planet X is coming is there really still hope?" I ask.

They don't hear me over the sound of the slots and bells and dings of the casino floor.

I leave the artist and the boy to their moment. I don't want to go back to my party. Not yet. I call Sarah.

"Hi, darling. Has Larry woken up yet?"

"No, Dad."

"You giving him water anyway?"

"Yes. You okay, Dad? You don't sound so good."

"Yeah, honey. Don't worry. I'm fine."

We hang up.

Planet X is heading toward Earth. Any time now it will pass the Kupier Belt then all the world will know.

I wanted to talk about it with Sarah one more time. Was hanging up a bad idea? Hosting a party in a Las Vegas Hotel during a tattoo art convention *is* a bad idea. That's for sure. So is leaving the state without the permission of your parole officer. But living canvases and SOHO rent for my gallery don't come cheap. Guess that doesn't matter anymore but I still need the world to know.

My parole officer didn't say I couldn't go to the Inked Nation

Convention. But she didn't say I could. I figure what she doesn't know can't hurt her or, better yet, me.

I want the artist (my ex-wife/Sarah's mom/my publisher) to publish the book of my tattoo designs. On skin. A book with pages made of skin, not paper. But instead of listening to me try and sell her the project, she's comforting the boy. Helping him find his shield. And probably making out with him. She can find a way to make the book of skin happen. She's the only one who can. She has to understand ink on paper and digital particles is just not the same.

I need to clear my mind. I walk through the next casino bar and head to the gathering area outside. A granite counter rings a fuel-fed fire pit. I push through the revolving doors and join the enthusiastic crowd drinking and talking in the fire glow. Apparently there is a convention of the society of tropical fish and reptile illustrators going on at the same time here, who knew? Everyone is talking about ink and reptiles and fish.

A woman is sitting cross-legged on one of the high chairs ringing the counter. She's alone. Her legs are long and thin. A black-and-white tattoo of a Gila monster adorns her upper thigh. She takes a cigarette from a box with a brand name I don't recognize. I bum a smoke and find myself talking with her about lizards. Then my book. Her accent tells me she's from Australia.

"The art is skin. Books are paper. It's not the same," I say to her. "My publisher says people don't care. I care. Do you care?"

"Why does it even matter to you?"

"Why would you say that?"

"No reason," she says.

"Do you know Planet X is coming?"

"What?"

"It's okay. *You do know.* Planet X is coming. I have to get this right before it does. You're the first person besides my publisher and daughter I've told."

"Yeah nice, but um, I'm not a person," she says. "But I like this conversation. So, even if I believe you, which I don't, why does it matter? Tell me."

"Planet X coming is even more of a reason to put my book on skin. It's not likely anyone will survive but if they do, my book, this art has to survive. Wait. Did you just say you're not a person?"

I think of Sarah telling me brumination is old. Born of countless generations of lizards conforming to cycles that were ancient when humans were just dawning.

Through the window I see the artist and the boy walking past the bar arm in arm inside the casino. The sports game on the TV set above the liquor bottles flashes off and is replaced with a newscast. The message Planet X is coming scrolls across the screen. The woman who is not a person nods affirmatively.

The television shows rocket launches. People rich and poor living out their bucket lists. Everything imaginable.

Demons have thrown off their disguises and are massing in

cities around the world. Only they look just like us in the news reports. There is a horde of these very ordinary-looking demons outside on the strip.

I run inside and catch up with the artist and the boy. All around casino "life" goes on. All these people, they either don't know or don't care or they've chosen to come here. The boy has calmed down and leaves us to go to the restroom. I look at my ex-wife but before I can speak she grabs my head and kisses me. It's a beautiful kiss. Like when I first kissed her at midnight on the New Year's Eve we first met. Slow. Patient. Full of promise. Her lips full and strong as I remember. Every brush against mine a message. A love story all our own. She pulls away.

"Now leave," she says. "I want to be alone with him for the end."

"Him. Really?"

"We've had our time. Now, go."

I never thought I'd kiss her again. I never thought I'd ever feel a connection like what we'd once had. I never thought I could create something as pure as Sarah. I never thought I could know pain as harsh as seeing my daughter depart for Planet X. Of seeing my wife, my ex-wife depart for just...nothing. I've been a walking ghost. A walking man of stone. Waiting for Larry to wake up. And waiting for ghosts.

I turn. Walk away. Planet X is coming. She's right. We've had our time. I know I'll never see her again.

The bar TV shows hordes of demons rampaging on the strip. All around me in the casino the masses are playing slots, oblivious or willfully disregarding what is happening.

The woman from the fire ring, the one who says she is not a person comes inside and watches the screen with me.

"Fuck it, the battle is lost," she says.

"That's it," I say. "That's all you have to say?"

"We'll just be called back to Gehana and get sent to some other planet. What about you? You have any regrets?"

"Regrets? Well. I've never gotten any tattoos," I say. "I guess that's not gonna happen now."

"That sounds like a regret. Why'd you never get any?"

"Never found one I wanted enough."

"What do you think you'd want?"

"Flowers," I say. "Something from Australia. Along with a bearded dragon. But I'd want it modeled from real life though and I never got around to it."

My phone rings.

"Hold on it's my daughter," I say.

Sarah tells me Larry is up.

"Give him water," I say. "And greens and those hornworms. I can't wait to see you it's been so long."

"It's been a day, Dad."

Does she not know Planet X is coming? Do I have to be the one to tell her?

"I love you," I say.

"Okay, Dad. Love you too."

We hang up.

"Want to hit the tables?" the demon woman asks.

"I guess. But not really."

"Me neither."

"I'm supposed to be hosting this party. I guess I should go up there and see that through. Then we can go do something if you want. Oh, and I want to call my parole officer and tell her to fuck off."

Back in the hotel room the party has thinned out but it's still going. My living canvases have gotten into my tattoo gear and are tattooing each other. A bunch of people are making out on the bed.

"Don't you all know Planet X is coming?" I yell.

Most everyone doesn't respond. One of my canvases looks up from her tattoo in progress and says, "Yeah, we do. We all do."

I shrug.

The demon woman shrugs.

We head to the parking garage for a car. In the garage she helps me boost a 1970 caramel brown Dodge Charger. It feels good to steal a car again. Besides tattooing it's the only thing I ever was really good at.

"What about you?" I ask. "Any regrets?"

"There was this one church," she says. "This congregation. They were ripe. I could have turned them all. Let's go there."

"Even if it doesn't matter?" I ask. "It's the end."

"What else can we do? Stay here? Rampage? Play slots?"

"I guess it's not too late to see my daughter. I should really go find my ex-wife and get her to publish my book of skin."

"You did say book of skin, right?"

"Yeah."

"Is it for eating?"

"No."

"Then what's it for?"

"Never mind. Doesn't matter. How many days you think we have left?"

She shrugs.

"You know the horde is out there," she says.

"You drive first shift or should I?" I reply.

I get in. The white vinyl interior feels like home. I start the ignition.

What about you? What do you want to do? Now that you know the truth about Planet X, what are you going to do? We're leaving. This ride is leaving. You coming?

THIS IS THE SOUND
OF YOUR DREAMS DYING

The sound of the end is one we all know.

The din of the crowd is silent for a heartbeat as I look up from my drink and notice her walking back to our table from the restrooms near the stage where they're setting up the band. The dim light has her backlit. Her round fur hat. Black, braided hair hanging over her shoulders and down her back. Jeans. Boots. Thin legs. Big, heavy sweater. Her silhouette and the sound of her voice are right out of my dreams but it's neither that has my heart racing.

I met her outside on the line. Out of nowhere she huddled up to me against the November cold and the uncaring Brooklyn faces and never left my side. She's unsteady on her feet from the drinks we've downed already but I know she's heading for me and that is all there is for her. Right now. Here. Our moments set to collide.

My dreams have been broken so many times before. Broken, knitted back together, and broken again so, so many times I can't remember where all the breaks are and what my younger self once contemplated a pristine and unmended notion of my life was supposed to be.

Tonight was supposed to be about taking this place back. Reclaiming it as part of my story. My story alone. I'd been meaning to check out this band, who I think has what it takes to...reach over...but didn't want to come because of my memories. And I didn't want to come alone. Ev knows how much this place means. What we experienced. So I called her. So much for letting go. I told myself that if she doesn't call back by ten, then that's it.

This morning when I woke up, if you had asked me I would have told you that I thought love was an unbroken line, a connection between two people, an uninterrupted tone stretching endlessly into the future. Everything that is you, everything that is her, vibrating together just right with the background sound of the universe, the wavelengths of color and light and sonics that surround us and everything. Love is felt in your bones. In your chest. In that place in you that does not seem to reside in your body yet comes alive, lucid and vital, when harmonics are hit.

This is a story about what happens after you hear that sound. The tragic change we detect by way of absence. The tones, the words, the physical vibrations through the air are different for everyone. Yet what happens is the same. Something we all know to be true, whether we have awareness of what we are experiencing or not. The sound of the end of love, the end of dreams is knowledge we all share.

The techies have done their final set up and left the stage. The hundred people milling about on the floor have moved to the front. There's room for more at the surrounding tables but there aren't that many people tonight.

My new friend retakes her seat.

I check my phone. Nothing.

"Waiting for someone?"

"No," I say. "Was possibly expecting an important call. But it's a sign, you know."

"A sign of what?"

"Of not to wait around. That I was right."

"Their loss, right," she says. She turns in her chair and looks over her shoulder at the stage. "I'm excited for tonight. I think they have what it takes."

"You do? Which one?"

"Not sure. I think the drummer."

"The drummer? Really? I've never seen it happen by a drummer..."

"I have," she says. "Sometimes lightning strikes twice."

I raise my glass to that.

"Another?" I ask. "What are you having?"

"I don't know," she says. "The gin and agave thing was good.

Good enough for another. But if it happens, I want to remember it. You come here a lot? What else is good that isn't going to knock me into oblivion?"

"I've only been here one time before," I say. "I don't know."

The night it happened was the night I had decided no more fucking around. I was going to step up and show Ev how much I loved her. In actions, not only words. So I'd brought my car to her house (it was still hers for at least a little while longer), parked it in her garage for once, and said I'd spend the night. That was what she wanted. Me there. And to feel like some semblance of a normal family unit. She had no idea in my trunk, locked in a case, was a handful of coins worth enough to make all her troubles disappear. At least her money troubles.

I was looking forward to feeling normal for once too; to having a carefree night out with my girl. Ev's sister was in from out of town and I had agreed to take them out and show them a good time. I knew there was a chance the band we were seeing could make it happen, but even if they could I didn't really think it was the time or the place. So I found myself out on the town, my recording gear left behind, relaxing despite myself.

The bouncer let us in and the host, a young guy, escorted us through a hall plastered with band posters. Ev and her sister, in between, giggling and ogling the guy, lamented that there was a time that they would have known each and every band. I knew them all. Didn't like them all but I knew of every player. Two mirrors flanked the walls where the hallway opened to the cavernous, warehouse-sized space that was the club. Ev checked her black ensemble, hiked her top up, and smoothed the lapels of her black velvet blazer that I loved on her so much.

She looked like an ambassador from hell. In all the right ways. She didn't get out much but when she did she liked to dress up. I preferred her with her just-woken-up-all-over-the-place hair and no makeup but she loved the black lipstick she had on. And the purple eye shadow. And how her mom-acceptable-length hair was sprayed straight up. I admit I liked her funky hairdo, but it was because it accentuated her face which I found so beautiful no matter how much makeup she wore.

Ev's sister, fresh off the plane from Belgium (where she had recently moved from Vienna with her new lover) was a legend out of my childhood. I grew up in the same suburban town as them, though I had never met her, Gwendolyn, Ev's notorious older sister. We figured out that I might have been in the same place as her once, one of their many our-parents-are-away house parties. These always ended in some sort of ruin or another. At one of these particularly mad nights I found myself in the bathroom and it seemed like everyone all at once was rushing in to flush their bags of pot and drugs because the cops were on the lawn. This girl came in and started rescuing the drugs from the toilet and then switched to just taking them from people. I'm told that was Gwen.

I'd heard of more of her exploits now and then during my

travels; how she had moved to Europe on a wing and a prayer, tales of her trails of broken hearts. Ev would spout Gwen's mad theories on life and love whenever she got really afraid, which was far too often lately. Being a divorced mom with kids and not much else in an increasingly scary world wasn't something too many people understood. I understood. Apparently Gwen understood despite never being married and never having kids. I felt something like pride when Ev first told me her sister, the legend, approved of me and said that I was a keeper. Gwen didn't look much like a legend right now. She looked like a world-weary girl in a black sweat suit who sort of looked like Ev, except for the extra weight, which I took was from living large for too long. They both couldn't hide the dark circles under their eyes. It was the tell-tale mark of the beyond burnt-out and over-extended I knew way too well from the faces of countless musicians caught in the never-ending cycle of teaching, studying, and gigs on top of all night practicing and rehearsals.

I'd managed to get off that train. My runaway ride around the world the long way landed me back home. I looked suburbs. I could even pass for suburbs. I had the comfort and stability the soft life brings, but I was not suburbs. I figured that was part of what Ev saw in me. I was a guy right there in the suburbs where she was struggling to raise her kids, only beneath the surface of clean-cut and stable I wasn't a part of it at all. I'd been around the world. To the borders of several more, and wound up choosing to come back where I started. A place she had never left and felt trapped in.

I was happy where I was. Relatively speaking. A big part of that was that I chose who I considered my family. As opposed to the fucked-up, pretzel twists of honor and guilt and wish fulfillment that made up most family dynamics I knew. Also I stayed away from most functions that included anyone's relatives, legendary or not. But Ev wanted to show me off to her sister, show *us* off—what we had—so I said okay to coming out.

The nightclub was nice. It had what seemed like real wood everywhere. The floorboards. The tables and stools. I could do without the ubiquitous TV screens running loops of artsy bits of seventies movies cut with the names of upcoming club events. Like "Lebowski-Fest."

"Oooh, Lebowski-Fest," Gwen said. "Now that's a movie."

"People get together and celebrate movies," I said. "That's a thing?"

"You haven't seen *The Big Lebowski*?" Gwen said.

"No," Ev and I said at the same time.

"Gross," Gwen said. "You two really are made for each other. Soulmates make me sick. See the movie. Together. It's a rare good one."

"Wanna go?" Ev asked. "Let's see it and then go? I want to."

"Sure," I said.

But I wasn't sure. I was feeling reckless for going out without my gear. But saying yes to her was akin to feeling like we were our pre-broken-up selves, which was a big part of what I saw in Ev. She saw me as my pre-broken-up self. Someone who was young, and smart, and full of potential. Even though back then we weren't an item, our paths crossed enough times for me to still have the phone number of the house she grew up in, in the little paper phone book I'd had since I was six. It was the one of the few nostalgic items I'd allowed myself to hold on to. Our teenage years were all about the search for fun and the search for knowledge and meaning and place and expansion of self in an endless string of after-school hangouts, backseats of cars, train rides, jaunts to the city, late-night movies, and dark and quiet suburban streets broken with our music and our conversations about the nature of everything.

Back then we didn't know that there was more to the world than what we saw. How could we? We didn't know fragility. Or pain. Or loss. Or how lucky we really were just by the nature of indulging in our oh-so-tragic teenaged existential struggles. The weight of what I know now is what gives me the sleepless nights and sometimes the dark circles. I can't un-know. I can't go back to sleep and be suburbs as much as I might want to at times and despite having tried once or twice.

"So this is Estelle's band," Gwen asked.

"Yeah," I said.

Estelle played the keyboards and sang harmonies. We went to school with her. She was the quiet girl. The new girl from far away. "Exotic" before it was a word used and misused for any number of connotations. Ev and I both had befriended her independently back then. Back then we were both guided by our compassion and compulsion to take in strays. Neither of us knew she had a twin until we reconnected with each other, and then with her when her band began to make a stir. What Thalia, her twin, had been doing or where she was during our high school years I never found out. I reconnected with Estelle when I came back from a treasure hunting expedition in Darwin a decade ago. A drummer I had met out there told me to look up Rex Francis's latest project; when I did there were Estelle and Thalia. Thalia sang lead and played rhythm guitar. Rex Francis played the lead guitar and wrote all the songs with Thalia. They had once been lovers and now were just best friends, or so Estelle said last I spoke to her. They all lived together. Something about Rex made me think there was a chance he could really make it happen. But how did he go on in a creative relationship with her? Was it something about that? Or had their relationship been something else all along that they had just called love?

Evie loved me. She was the first person who had ever said the words who I believed. I more than believed. I knew for sure. Her actions defined the concept for me and shined a glaring light on the falseness and mistakes, on everything else and everyone that had come before. She was the end of the hurt. The justification for why I had gone on. Why I had hung in there all these years. She was the only person I believed in. There were spaces in her life that I was able to fill. Able to fill by becoming a stronger, more compassionate version of myself.

She loved me so much that soon after we got together she declared that I alone would be her only lover. Something about her feelings for me transcended the carnal. Seems like a given but this was a first for her. Her life, despite her marriage, had been filled with and defined by lust. Her body craved physical pleasure, overwhelming, all-encompassing physical pleasure. I understood that sex and earthly delights were the only way she could silence her mind. It was the only respite she had from the pain and responsibility she found herself in. Responsibility she was never quite up for and never quite lived up to, despite spending all her time trying.

She adored me for just being me. Being me mostly consisted of being there through her work all-nighters (getting other people's parties ready), helping make ends meet (I did all the shopping and most of the cooking), and being there for her as her soon-to-be ex-husband slowly but surely out-maneuvered her (her almost-over divorce cost her the house that her children had grown up in and her savings).

All the moments where she would have otherwise been alone I was there. It was during these moments when she realized how fragile everything was and how stability and security were just illusions and fairy tales to keep those who had to keep on moving, moving. Thinking about it now I wonder if what she saw in me had something to do with me being an anchor to her life before, a connection to herself before life went wrong for her. Maybe her love for me had a lot less to do with me than I'd like to believe.

Our server brought menus.

"Sliders? This is what you eat here in the States now," Gwen said. "Why no burgers?"

"Fuck you," Ev said. "Sliders rule. I'm having sliders and the vodka and St. Germain with grapefruit puree and agave syrup thing."

"Oh dear," Gwen said.

The food. The drink. The carelessness of the moment and lack of consequence of the decision at hand felt decadent. I loved to see Ev laugh and have someone around her besides me who gave a damn.

Ev's phone rang. I could tell by the deflated look it was her kids. She barked orders about food and laundry and homework into the phone before Gwen grabbed it, shut it off, and refused to give it back.

"You have a sitter," Gwen said. "The sky won't fall. You deserve an hour or two. For yourself. With your sister you never see."

Before Ev could reply, and I could tell she was about to give her sister an earful, the house lights cut and the music started.

A single ethereal synthesizer tone floated through the darkness—a warbled approximation of a human voice transposed through analog circuits. The drums came in with a basic beat underneath, good old-fashioned, real drums. I could hear the pedal strike the kick drum and the stick strike the snare. Then the single tone blurred into an angelic wash of tones. The drummer broke into sixteenth notes on the hi-hat as the guitars came in. No bass. Somehow the keyboards and guitars and everything else filled out the bottom.

I didn't think the band would start with this song. It was about a ship. A ship a long, long way from home lost in a storm at sea. And a sailor who realizes because of his choice to follow the sea it is becoming more and more likely he'll never see his wife again.

A pretty old-fashioned notion but the song was anything but old-fashioned. The music sounded like the music of the future. Of the future I'd always wanted. A bit electronic, yes, but progressed without being progressive. There was nothing flashy or synthetic about the sound, yet it was so fresh and refreshing and original. I felt inspiration in the performance. The fleeting notion that anything was possible. Despite the shit that I had to wade through before and the shit to be waded through after, I felt happy, and in the presence of something profound and meaningful even if the only meaning I could pin down was artistic expression of uncommon purity and quality.

Ev and Gwen turned to each other and an expression that I could only interpret as "fuck this" passed between them. They had heard a call in the music that they recognized and shared with the secret knowledge of sisters. They answered by downing their drinks, pushing out of their stools, and bee-lining for the floor. I followed. I was welcome, but not part of the equation. It no longer mattered if I was with them or caught up with them later or whatever. It wasn't an exclusionary thing. They were going to be part of this the best way they knew how, by dancing and by getting real close.

Estelle and Thalia came in together on vocals. And the chills hit me. Something hidden in my nervous system came alive with sensations that shot up the back of my legs to my shoulders. Their harmonies killed me. They had some flange and reverb going on but the sound wasn't wet. It was the magic of singers, the magic of sisters doing it the old-fashioned way, by locking in and translating intent and emotion through intervals of sound. Musical alchemy. They sang of being lost at sea and I was lost at sea with them.

Gwen and Ev half-danced, half-pushed through the crowd. I struggled to stay near but settled for keeping them in my line of sight. There was no bass player but Estelle was hitting the low keys of her synth and Rex was playing an arpeggio pattern of open chords that was evolving and folding over and over itself. My chest vibrated with each start of the cycle. Estelle caught my eye as she hit a low note with her left hand. I responded with the facial expression that said "I'm feeling it" that all musicians recognize.

Ev and Gwen danced at the front with the excited crowd. Estelle and Thalia harmonized perfectly on the final lyric, which left it unclear if the lovers ever saw each other again. I figured they'd either transition into another song or play right into the next song on the album.

But the song did not end. They started the pattern again. The drummer dug in. I was close enough to hear the unamplified kick drum and wooden sticks on the forged metal cymbals drawing the song forward into unknown territory.

They were playing through. They weren't stopping. The bass notes altered the chords, lifting the song away from the melancholy toward something more insistent and kinetic. Rex stopped playing his rhythm pattern and I heard the guts of the song. Thalia. Estelle. The drummer keeping the shape recognizable while folding it into something new. Rex came back in with a single, mournful note. It evoked the first note that had opened the song; the perfect start to a lead. Quiet. Confident. Simple. Bold. He was taking his time working into a solo over this new iteration of the song.

The sound was perfect. I couldn't figure out who was playing what. The low end resonated like a heavy bell. Was someone ringing a bell? I wasn't sure.

Rex's eyes were closed. His hands on the fretboard and strings leading him, leading us, where the solo was taking him.

Estelle was looking into the audience and singing. She wasn't on the mike but she was singing the words of the song. I could tell. Thalia had her back to the crowd and was locked in with the drummer, weaving the driving, steady backbone. Rex held his notes and let them resonate above Estelle's chords that moved from dissonant to heavenly and back again.

Something fell on me. I swatted my face and flicked away a small piece of glass. I touched my cheek and found a drop of blood on my finger. I looked up and saw the house lights were off. The one above me had shattered. Something else fell, bounced off my head, and disappeared into the mess of legs and boots and darkness of the crowded floor. A small stick, I thought. I looked around and noticed everyone in the place, waitresses, bouncers, bartenders, had gathered around the floor to watch. That's when I realized Rex had it in him and thought he might actually pull it off.

I heard the bell before I saw it.

The song was lifting higher and higher. Rex's lead weaving deeper into the inversions. Adding notes and colors into the patterns which felt more complex, darker, more significant as each cycle of measures progressed. Binding it all was that low, steady tone, what I can only think of as being the intoning of a great bell. And then I saw it there before me. Above the stage. A bell. Three feet high. A steeple-like housing materialized around it. Then I realized the housing was mounted on the hull of a ship. Like a prop in some Broadway show there was now a ship where seconds ago the back of the club used to be. Only it wasn't there. I could sort of make out the back wall through it. No one, certainly not the band, was reacting to its appearance at all.

Rex's eyes remained closed. Ev turned around and smiled and nodded to me, and for the last time I could remember she communicated with me with just an expression. We both knew what we were looking at. What we had been searching for so many times before was now before us. Proof. Only I didn't have a stitch of gear. It didn't matter. I knew it would matter later but all that mattered just then was the truth of the moment.

Something hit my head again. I looked up at the lights to make sure they weren't falling or something.

I couldn't believe Rex was still going. Ev and Gwen danced on as the ship became more and more tangible with the deepening of Rex's lead. Then I saw the drummer had stopped and felt the difference in the sound before I realized whatever beat I was hearing was not coming from the drums on the stage. Thalia had stopped playing her guitar. She had it slung around her back and was behind the kit helping the drummer. She lifted him off his stool and he hung limply in her arms. The bell tone filled the space where her rhythm parts had been; something less, yet so much more than what she had been playing—something terribly wrong, yet intriguingly perfect for the new iteration of the song Rex and Estelle were driving.

Something hit me yet again. I ran my hand along the top of my head. It was coated with blood. Glass and sticks were falling from somewhere above. I picked up a piece of the debris.

It wasn't a stick. It was a bone. A finger bone. Wet with blood and brown, sinewy gristle.

Rex's eyes opened. The expression on his face read bliss but his eyes screamed "help me." He wasn't stopping. I didn't think he could stop.

The crowd degenerated into a mob pushing and rushing to exit around those still watching the band unfazed. Ev and Gwen were up in my face.

"Come on," Ev said. "We're out of here."

How could she want to leave? This was what we'd always hoped for. What we'd stayed up countless nights dreaming of.

I looked at Gwen. Ev and I were about to have a meltdown and she knew it. Was she enjoying it?

Ev was screaming something at me but my focus was on the stage behind her. I could no longer see through the ship. There were people on board. I couldn't make them out as more than just person-like shapes. Except for one. A woman. Standing on the bow striking the bell with a mallet. Everything about her was familiar, though I couldn't focus on any part of her. I knew that I knew her and that she was a woman striking a bell.

"I can't go now," I said.

"Show's over," Ev said. "We're going. Now."

"I don't think he can stop," I said. "I think he's in trouble."

A bone that could have been a human femur fell on the head of the girl behind Ev who stood rapt at the performance.

"Fuck this," Ev said. "This is bad. I can't get hurt here."

I recognized the truth in her words. Throughout our lives we'd broken rules. Together and alone we'd gotten away with things. Out-maneuvered cops and parents and all sorts of authorities for tons of different reasons. I knew her so well that I knew exactly what she meant. If she perished or got hurt here, she feared what would become of her kids. I knew what came along with that even though it remained unsaid. She couldn't count on me. But I was ready. Ready to be there. All the way. Yet she didn't know. How could she? I hadn't told her.

"What about Rex?" I said.

Wasn't anyone going to help him?

"I'm going up there," I said.

Gwen laughed. I realized she didn't care one way or another what happened so long as the party rolled on. And the party was rolling on, our fight her main attraction now.

I ran past them and onto the riser that was the stage. Bones and glass were raining on the remaining audience. I didn't know what was happening. Rex was a man transfixed. A man lost.

His eyes said I am a prisoner.

I pulled at the plug running from his guitar to his pedal board severing the signal to his amp. After a few seconds the majestic tone ceased and there was only an echo of his last notes carrying over Estelle's keyboard line and the bell.

Rex collapsed. Estelle stopping playing and ran across the stage to us.

Cops were here, weaving their way through the floor to us. The ship was gone. Only a haze in the air where it had been remained. When the first officer reached us there was nothing left at all.

Gwen and Ev were gone too. I tried to help the EMTs bring Rex to one of the ambulances outside but they kept me away.

They questioned me about the bones. Even showed me one in a plastic evidence bag.

"What is this evidence of?" I asked.

The bone looked broken and healed and re-broken. They didn't know. And after I'd answered all their questions I was free to go and they moved on to the next one to be questioned.

I went straight to the hospital to visit Rex.

Estelle was with him. He lay in a bed. Motionless. Eyes closed.

"They say nothing's wrong with him," Estelle said. "He's not even dehydrated or anything rock and roll like that."

"What the hell happened to him?"

"He won't wake up," she said. "They say his brain waves are like he's sleeping."

"You were on the stage. What do you think?"

"I don't know. I guess you can't play like that without consequences."

Consequences? Was that the best she had? I wanted her to say that they knew something I didn't. That they knew something supernatural. Or a scientific theory about the quantum nature of things. Or that they inadvertently or even intentionally hit on the right code to open a door. They were the best of us and were still just like monkeys tapping at typewriters.

"Where are Thalia and Ed?"

"Gone," she said. "Thalia says she's done."

"Done?"

"With the band."

"What? She quit? Just like that?"

"Said she's going somewhere far away with Simone and never coming back."

"Who's Simone?"

"The drummer."

"Right," I said. "Does Rex have family?"

"Me. I guess," she said.

"What about health insurance?"

"Um, maybe. No. I don't think so. Our label is in France. I should put a call in to them."

"I'm gonna stay. I'll help."

"What can you do that I can't?"

"I don't know," I said. "I can be here. You can't be here twenty-four/seven."

"Twenty-four/seven? He's gonna be fine."

It didn't seem like he was going to be fine. My heart told me his body was here but that Rex was somewhere out at sea.

My phone rang.

It was Gwen.

"My sister's freaking out. Get over here," she said.

"What. What's wrong?"

"She can't find her youngest kid."

"How do you lose an eight-year-old?"

"I don't know just shut up and get your ass here now."

A "sold" sticker was plastered over the For Sale sign in front of Ev's big house in the burbs that was hers for just a little while longer. Almost everything inside was packed up. The sheriff was set to come any day now and she didn't have a plan.

She didn't know that what I had in my car I figured was enough for a down payment on a new house in the same neighborhood or one close enough.

Ev, Gwen, and the sitter, a teenage girl, were out on the porch, smoking.

"What happened?" I asked.

"I told you. The youngest kid is missing," Gwen said.

"His name's Charlie," Ev said. "Why don't you call my son by his name for a change?"

I reached for her but she wouldn't look at me. I turned to the sitter.

"The oldest is upstairs playing video games," the teenage girl said.

"Smoking?" I asked.

"Yeah," she said.

"Alone?" I asked.

"Yes. But the middle one was out back in the yard necking with her boyfriend all night."

"On a school night," I said.

Ev glared at me.

"So where's Charlie?" I asked.

"I couldn't find him," the sitter said. "Then they came home."

I thought I heard a tone that sounded like the opening note of the song but maybe was just a train in the distance. I played the floor plan of the house through my mind's eye and asked them if they checked each room as I pictured it. When I got to the unfinished guest room adjoining the house, the room where all of her ex's stuff was awaiting pickup, I figured I knew where Charlie was.

"Did you check in the guest room?" I asked.

"He's not in there," Ev said. "I keep it locked."

She was always averse to the room. I had been the one who had moved all the boxes myself.

"Keys please," I said.

After a fuss Gwen brought the keys. I opened the door and looked in. The boxes were still piled where I'd left them and yes there was Charlie sitting on one and talking to someone. It was dark but I could see Charlie just fine. The person stood next to him cloaked in shadow. Was it a woman? I thought so but couldn't be sure. Something about her was familiar. Whoever she was she didn't belong here.

"Gwen, bring me a knife from the kitchen," I said.

"Gwen don't," Ev said.

"Bring it," I said.

I hated how I had growled the words. I rarely yelled. When I did it was ugly. This was the first time I could recall using the tone in front of Ev.

Gwen disappeared and returned with a kitchen knife. I took it from her.

"I'm going in. Stay here," I said.

"My child is in there," Ev said.

I couldn't argue. She and Gwen followed as I slowly walked toward Charlie and the person.

"Hi," Charlie said as we approached.

I could see the person with him better. It *was* a woman. She sat on one of the big boxes of stuff across from Charlie. I tried to place where I knew her from but I couldn't figure out if she was young or old, or even discern anything about her at all.

"What're you doing, Charlie?" I asked.

"Talking," he said.

"To who?"

"Her."

With his words I saw the woman before him was the woman who had been striking the bell on the stage. There was a terrible moth-ball, formaldehyde smell about her. I realized that I shouldn't be trusting my eyes but I was sure this was her. Whose body she was wearing, however, I had no idea.

"What do you see?" I asked Gwen.

"You mean the old lady?"

"What does she look like?"

"Not so good. Like death."

"You did this," Ev said. "She…it followed you here. You helped Rex and now she's here because of you."

"Quiet, please," I said. "I'm going to handle this. Please just let me."

"Hi, Charlie," I said nice and slow. "Who is this with you?"

He said a name. The word was incomprehensible. I hadn't been afraid until I heard Charlie say it.

"She says everything's okay. She knows you," he said. "She said she's going to take me on a boat. You too."

"What the fuck did you bring to my house?" Ev said to me. "Do something."

How did this become my fault? I wanted to tell her not to worry, that it was a good sign that this thing was wearing the body of someone old. Someone weak. Maybe someone recently dead. It meant whatever it was, it wasn't strong, yet, and that I might have a chance. I knew that much. Didn't change what I had to do.

Ev rushed for her child. And Gwen, bless her wild heart, grabbed her sister and stopped her.

"Let me the fuck go," she said. "I'm taking my son."

The corpse, or old woman, or the woman from the stage, whoever the hell it was, slowly moved her hand onto Charlie's shoulder in response. I didn't like how otherwise silent and motionless she remained, despite our presence.

"Ev. I'm going to fix this. Just let me focus here. Gwen, take her out of the room, please."

Gwen led Ev by the arm back to and through the door. Ev was full of fight and curses, but her older sister knew how to handle her and wasn't afraid to do so.

When I heard the door close I slowly moved closer to the woman and Charlie. As I stepped next to them, the woman opened her mouth and started to say something.

I stabbed her in the neck before she could. It didn't matter.

Whatever she had to say couldn't matter. As much as I wanted to hear, as much as I yearned to know if she had any answers for my questions, I knew whatever she had to say led to ruin. She didn't belong here. She only wanted skin. A body. An approximation of life. Whatever Rex had done, or whatever I had done, if it was even us at all, was not right. She was a thing that should not be. But she was here.

I stabbed her again. Her hand remained on Charlie.

"Are you hurting her?" Charlie asked.

"No, I'm not hurting her," I said.

I stabbed her in her stomach. Her hands. Her legs. I wasn't sure how much she could take. Finally her hand slid off Charlie's shoulder and I pushed her.

Charlie's face was full of tears. Poor kid was used to people lying. Was used to pretending he believed the lies, but even this was too much for him.

"She said she'd take me on a boat to a new home," he said. "My dad says that too sometimes. Did you do that to my dad too?"

"No, this lady was going to hurt you."

"Mom says Dad wants to hurt us."

"I don't know what to say right now, little man. Other than sometimes bad things happen. But you have family. Family are people who stick together when bad things happen."

"You gonna stick with us?"

"Yeah. I'm gonna stick with you. Starting now," I said. "Just gotta tell your mom."

I gently walked Charlie to the door, opened it, and sent him through to Ev's waiting embrace. She was relieved but oh so furious with me. There was a dumpster outside but no way that would do for this mess. I had a long night ahead of me.

"Give me a day," I said. "I'll take care of this and then I'll be back."

"Where are you going? What are you going to do?" Ev asked.

"There are places. Don't ask. Listen," I said and handed her my keys. "I'm gonna get started but in my car there is a case. Inside are some coins. They're worth enough to make sure everything's going to be all right."

"What? Money?" she asked.

"Sort of money. It's worth a lot."

"Wait. You had this all along?"

"Well, I guess, yes."

"I could have saved the house? I could have saved the house with it?"

"Nothing was going to save this house. There's nothing here but dead dreams and now...this. You guys can start new. We all can. Together."

"Lucky you, sis," Gwen said. "I told you he was a keeper."

Ev didn't look at me as she hugged Charlie even tighter.

When I came back from getting rid of the body, Ev and the kids were gone. Most of her stuff was still there. No one had bothered to clean the bloodstains.

Gwen lay on the couch next to a spilled bag of Chex party mix and what looked like an open ziplock full of cocaine. Two people who might have been men, or a man and a very masculine woman, were passed out on the floor at her feet. It was a far pathetic cry from the legendary parties of our youth but it was the remnants of a party nonetheless.

"Where is she, Gwen?"

Gwen opened her eyes. After a second, recognition rose through her drugged-out gaze.

"I don't know. If I did, I wouldn't tell you."

"I'll find her."

"I'm sure you can. I'll know where she is once she settles. But she doesn't want you to find her. So why would you?"

"She took my money."

"You took her life. And no, you *gave* her that money."

"*I* took her life?"

"She didn't take you to that club. She didn't knife an old lady in your guest house in front of *your* eight-year-old."

"I can't believe this."

"Wait. No. She didn't take all the money."

Gwen handed me one of my coins.

"It's only right," she said. "She left two. Sorry, I used one. Man, blow is expensive here."

"I'm going to find her," I said.

But already I doubted myself.

"My bet is after you think about it, you won't go looking. Not if you know what's good for you."

"What's that supposed to mean? Are you threatening me?"

"No, I'm helping you. She's done. You're done. Listen, I know you didn't ask me but you, all of you, think love is forever. But it's not. Why would it be? We're not forever. We're fragile. And temporary."

"Like a flower, man," the man on the floor mumbled.

"Yes," Gwen said a little too emphatically. "Like a flower. Love has a cycle. A lifespan. An expiration date."

"Like a flower," the man said again.

I ran out of the room, out of the house. I wanted to throw the three of them out onto the street but I couldn't stay a second longer.

The new girl clicks my glass and we sip the murky white drinks glowing in the club's soft lights. I taste just a hint of what I know is very strong alcohol beneath the tart bite and sweetness.

"Well, ching-ching," she says. "Here's to tonight."

"To tonight," I say.

"You never know what can happen."

She's right. She has no idea how so very right she is. And I'm not going to tell her. Certainly not now. She's wonderful but she's a possibility. A hope. My rainbow. I know that sounds cruel but when you've been cut to nothing, when your guts are tangled on the razor-glass shards of your broken life you can either just rip yourself up or pull out and go on. Pretend to be whole until the day comes that you are pretending no longer.

I thought I was telling you about the sound of dreams dying. And maybe I have. I think I stumbled onto something else though. Something like that bass line. Something I can't localize, point out, or even really hear. Maybe it's the static of an amplified guitar disconnecting. Maybe it is the sound of an empty house or the nothing at the other end of Ev's phone number I called earlier even though I know it's been disconnected.

Maybe the sound is the emptiness of space waiting to be expanded into. Almost undetectable. Almost imperceptible. A leaf unfurling. A flower opening. Another bone mending. Yeah, the sound of the end we all know. But what about that of another moment beginning? What about that? Do you know? Can you hear it?

The new girl turns toward the stage and from her hair I catch a hint of something floral and white, something comforting and alluring I last smelled long ago when I was young.

The house lights cut and a song I think I know starts.

-

ABOUT THE AUTHOR

Daniel Braum is the author of *The Night Marchers and Other Strange Tales* (Cemetery Dance Publications/Grey Matter Press, 2016) and *Yeti. Tiger. Dragon.* (Dim Shores, 2016). The collection *Yeti. Tiger. Dragon. Leopard.* is forthcoming from Necon E-Books.

His fiction has most recently appeared in or is forthcoming in *Space and Time Magazine* (issue #127, December 2016), *Would but Time Await* (Orford Parish Books, 2017) and *Nightscripts 3* (C. M. Mueller, 2017).

He is the host of the Night Time Logic reading series in New York.

The short stories of Karen Russel, Robert Aickman, Kelly Link, Tanith Lee, and Lucius Shepard are among his favorites.

PRAISES FOR THE AUTHOR

"Divergent. Unlike anything else I'm reading today. Bold, adventurous, strange, and totally enjoyable."

– Frank Errington Michaels / Cemetery Dance

"Braum has a knack for describing the indescribable…"

– Teresa Delucci / Tor.com

"Full of sadness, beauty, and unprecendented wonder. Two cups of literary dark fiction, a heaping scoop of magical realism and urban fantasy, a tablespoon of horror. Yet these genres only scratch the surface…"

-- Chad Stroup / Subvertia

"…unflinching willingness to take on sensitive issues…One of the brightest young starts in the firmament of dark speculative fiction, Daniel Braum is among the best short story writers we've encountered."

-- Shane Douglas Keene / Shotgun Logic

"..well-crafted character-driven storytelling that is serving, and will continue to serve, Daniel Braum well as he continues to make a name for himself in the genre."

-- Thomas Joyce / This Is Horror

"Daniel Braum is the real deal, a writer to treasure. A real storyteller"

-Victor LaValle, author of The Ballad of Black Tom

"Daniel Braum's stories feel at once familiar and strange, exotic and dangerous or maybe just dangerously personal."

-David Wellington, Author of Monster Island

"Braum presents our world through a lens that reveals the wonderful and the horrifying with masterful, elegant prose"

-Lee Thomas, Lambda Literary Award and Bram Stoker Award-winning author.

"Faithless women and adventuring lone wolves populate Braum's trippy, fantastical stories of music, magic, and the search for connection. Take some Neil Gaiman, a dash of Kevin Brockmeier, and a whole lot of Long Island garage band, and stir."

-Sarah Langan – Bram Stoker Award winning author.

"I give very few quotes. I only make exceptions when a novel or collection knocks me out. So...short and sweet: buy Dan Braum's The Night Marchers. It's good, damn good. This man has one hell of a career ahead of him, and you get to be at the party before everyone else.

-Jack Dann -multiple award winning author and editor

ACKNOWLEDGEMENTS

Thank you to Alessandro Manzetti for being the Wish Mechanic who saw something dark and beautiful first in "How to Make Love and Not Turn to Stone" and then believed in this book with his poetic heart, strong enough to bring it to life.

To my family for everything. Especially to my father, the finest Wish Mechanic I have ever known.

Thank you, to my friends, teachers, colleagues, and readers.

Leslie What. Karen Joy Fowler. Tim Powers. Terry Bisson. Alice Turner. Marc Rudolph. Rudi Dornemann. Brendan Day. Sharon Woods. Catherine Holm. Nicholas Kaufmann. Chandler Klang-Smith. MM Devoe. Ben Francisco. John Foster. Jon Lees. David Wellington. Sarah Langan. Lee Thomas. Stefan Petrucha. Victor LaValle. Peter Ball. JJ Irwin. Chris Lynch. *Kaleidetrope Magazine.* Sam Cowen and Dim Shores Press. Norman Prentiss, Richard Chizmar, Brian Freeman, and the Cemetery Dance team. Dallas Mayr. Peter Straub. Jason Sileo. Marc Laidlaw. Scott Nicolay. Jack Dann. Ellen Datlow. Matthew Kressel. KGB Bar. Tonya Hurley. Morbid Anatomy Museum. The team at Independent Legions.

Thank you to beloved authors Lucius Shepard and Tanith Lee for being my gateways into the world of the fantastic. I wish I could have shared this book with you both.

Thank you all for reading my stories and for your support. This book is my wish come true thanks to you.